Angels

of

Redemption

Book 1

§

Written By
Alethea J Salazar

Text copyright © 2009 by Alethea J. Salazar
Cover Design by Alethea J. Salazar
Interior Design by Alethea J. Salazar

Library of Congress: TXU001700492
Printed in the United States of America
US Trade Paper
ISBN-10: 1448638933
ISBN-13: 978-1448638932
Fiction / Fantasy / Epic

§

REVISED EDITION 2011

Dedication

~ ---------------------- ~

For my husband, Greg and my dad Ralph
for always believing in my crazy ideas.

§

For my sister, Shondra and
my dear friend, Karen
for being my most loyal readers.

§

For my four sons,
Jake, Nick, Gabriel and Sterling
for always believing I'm the greatest
mom in the world... no matter what

§

And last but not least,
for my mom, Chandel for
helping to inspire the story...
Gone but not forgotten

DEAN KOONTZ CALLED ANGELS OF REDEMPTION "...INTERESTING SPIRITUAL FICTION - AND I'M RATHER INTO THAT MYSELF!"

"GREAT BOOK!!! ONCE I STARTED, I COULDN'T PUT IT DOWN. VINCHETTO IS THE MAN!!!"

5 STAR AMAZON READER REVIEW

"THIS IS A VERY COMPELLING STORY...IT BROUGHT OUT MANY EMOTIONS IN ME...I ANXIOUSLY AWAIT THE SEQUEL..."

5 STAR AMAZON READER REVIEW

"I COULDN'T PUT IT DOWN ONCE I STARTED READING...THIS WILL MAKE FOR A GOOD MOVIE ONCE THE RIGHT PERSON READS IT."

5 STAR AMAZON READER REVIEW

§

CONTENTS

~ -------------------- ~

INTRODUCTION

The guardians watched over their *mortal* with unfaltering determination. Despite their efforts to save her from herself, they had to accept the fact that her ultimate destiny would be determined by her own hand. This temporal realm in which she barely existed anymore was so thick with despair it was like treading water. She was in real trouble and nothing in the guardians' powers seemed to be helping her. She truly believes she is alone in this world and has nothing to lose. But her guardians would not give up. They never give up on one of their *mortals*.

Ever!

"Vinchetto, I don't know what to do. Nothing we say or do seems to be affecting her."

"I know Calista, but we don't quit. You know that," replied Vinchetto. His accent is thick and his voice deep, reassuring Calista and counteracting her unrelenting trepidation with every syllable. She likes being partnered up with him whenever she gets the chance. He's strong, fearless and hell-bent on saving everyone. They don't get much tougher than Vinchetto. Even the *soldiers* and the *higher levels* that are all too often present at their assignments fear him.

"How come the *soldiers* aren't doing anything?" Calista asked.

"'Cause they think they're going to win," he replied. Circling above their *mortal* were three vile beasts sent to cause as much unrest and despair as possible. Somehow the *soldiers* knew they would win this one. Vinchetto hoped that wasn't the case, it isn't in his nature to lose. Especially to the foul, contemptible minions of Hell.

Their *mortal,* a young woman named Sarah, was completely oblivious to her house guests as they followed her from room to room. She couldn't see them or hear them, and she couldn't feel them when they touched her. But somehow she sensed the emotions that radiated from them... including the *soldiers.*

She was overwhelmed with conflicting emotions. Angry, sad and desperate one minute, calm and peaceful the next, she didn't know what to do. She missed her family so much, that's all she could focus on anymore. It completely consumed her.

Her son and her husband were killed in a car accident and she was left completely alone. No family to dilute the heavy burden of her grief and help her survive this unthinkable tragedy. And now this beautiful thirty-two year old woman was ready to end it all just so she could be with her family again.

Calista and Vinchetto weren't going to let that happen, not on their watch. They were bound and determined to do everything in their power to stop her. But that task wasn't going to be so easy. Sarah had nothing to lose at this point... except her soul.

Unfortunately, Sarah wouldn't realize the price she would have to pay until it was too late, and Calista and Vinchetto had no way to tell her. All they could do was try to influence Sarah and hope they would win over the wretched *soldiers* as they instilled fear and doubt into her fragile heart and mind.

The battle for Sarah's soul was on, and the price was just too high. Calista and Vinchetto knew this, but in the end Sarah's *free will* would determine tonight's events and their ultimate outcome.

They all followed Sarah as she wandered into her bathroom. She started the tub and then began taking pills out of the medicine cabinet. After spending time with Sarah, watching her, influencing her and comforting her, despite all their efforts they were failing... and they knew it.

"Vinchetto!" yelled Calista. "We have to stop her!"

"I know Calista," he replied. He knew she was approaching the point of no return. They both watched as she began emptying all the pill bottles on the counter, one by one.

"Sarah, don't do this baby!" cried Vinchetto. Sarah couldn't hear him, but she could feel something inside her wanting to stop. She stared at the pills scattered on the counter.

"That a girl! Dump them in the sink now, you don't need those," continued Vinchetto. Calista held Sarah's face gently in her hands, trying to give her as much peace and comfort as she could. Calista pleaded with her to hang on.

The *soldiers* circled above her and were growing more agitated by the minute. They began to screech and plunged at her through the air. Vinchetto drew his sword and cut through the room, taking out two of the *soldiers*. They vanished into a burst of black smoke and dust, but one still remained. The beast fed Sarah's mounting despair, shrouding her with doubt and pain. It was now or never, the doubt inside her was seizing control. She scooped up a handful of pills and swallowed them. She grabbed another handful, and then another.

"No, no, no, no!" cried Calista, tears were pouring down her face. "Oh no Vinchetto, she did it!"

"I know kid... I know," said Vinchetto. He put his arms around Calista to comfort her. It's never easy to lose a *mortal* and Calista always takes it so hard. They want to save everyone, but that's not always a reality. No matter how hard they try, *free will* always wins.

Once a *mortal* has given up hope, they don't recover easily from their despair... if ever. Sarah had passed the point of no return. She had completely given up on herself and now her fate was sealed. The inevitable succession of her actions was out of her hands... and her guardians'. It was in God's hands now.

"Look," observed Calista. "The *soldier's* gone."

"Its work here is done, there's nothing else we can do," he replied. "We're going to stay until the end, ok?"

"Ok."

"It's not over Calista, we'll have another chance to save her. We couldn't save her tonight, but we'll make it right in the end."

"Talk to Nigel when we get back. Make sure she stays with us," said Calista.

"I will. We'll save her kid... I promise," said Vinchetto. They both sat with Sarah as she slowly slipped away. "I promise."

CHAPTER 1

The house was dark. There was no TV on, no radio. The only light burning was in Sarah Bradley's bedroom.

Sarah sat in an old armchair in the corner of her bedroom. It was the same chair her husband, Will, used to toss his clothes on every night when he changed for bed. The overstuffed armchair that once served as the final resting place for Will's laundry now cradled the tired body and fragile soul of Sarah Bradley. In her lap she held a picture of Will and their son Joey from some distant Christmas morning. Will had on a Santa hat and a pair of boxing gloves. Joey was wearing Tigger pajamas, and a matching pair of boxing gloves that were too big for his tiny hands. They were posed as if they were in the Heavy Weight fight of the Century.

Sarah caressed the silver "Merry Christmas Mommy" frame. She held it to her face and kissed it as tears streamed down her cheeks. She moved the picture to her chest and began to cry uncontrollably as she rocked back and forth, back and forth.

Through the unstoppable tears she was shedding she called out into the empty room, "I miss you so much!"

She said these words over and over again. Sarah screamed at the top of her voice and then was reduced to sobs again. She collapsed on the floor clutching the picture tightly to her chest and just kneeled there, face buried in the carpet.

"Please, dear God... why? Why did you take them from me? Let me come home... please! I'm begging you, let me come home! I don't want to be here anymore! Please God... please!"

The despair was like a vacuum. She couldn't stop the spiraling pain that consumed every inch of her. It had been three months since the accident, but the pain only grew worse.

There was no comfort in sight for Sarah as she fell deeper and deeper into a black pit of crippling despair. Free falling out of control into her awaiting prison of pain and loneliness.

Her *Hell*...

ζ

"Hi honey, we're on our way home," Will said on the phone.

"Hi mommy! The movie was awesome!" Joey yelled from the backseat.

"So I guess he loved the movie, huh?" asked Sarah. This, of course, was a rhetorical question.

"Of course! Who wouldn't love a movie about a lonely robot who can only say his own name over and over and over?" replied Will with a laugh.

"I take it you don't share your son's enthusiasm."

"Actually, the movie was great. It was really cute, you would have loved it," replied Will.

"I'll wait for the DVD, I wouldn't want to intrude on 'guy's night out'."

"No doubt, you might cramp our style when we're trying to pick up chicks!"

"Yeah… chicks!" Joey chimed in from the backseat. Will laughed.

"Whatever Rico Suave'. See you when you get home," laughed Sarah.

"10-4 babe. Love you."

"Love you too," she said.

"Love you too mommy!" yelled Joey.

"Love you too baby!" she answered.

"Hey, mommy says 'love you too'," Will relayed the message to Joey in the backseat. "See you soon babe," and then Will was gone.

ζ

Sarah picked herself up off the floor. She went into the bathroom and washed her face. She stood there for what seemed like an eternity just staring at the face in the mirror, but Sarah didn't recognize the woman staring back at her.

She had barely eaten since the accident, she hadn't worked. She hadn't even left the house since the funeral. In fact she seldom even bathed anymore. Sarah Bradley was no longer able to function in everyday life what-so-ever. She swears if she had to think to breathe she would probably stop doing that too. Depression had its teeth in her and wasn't letting go any time soon.

Sarah was nothing more than a shadow of the woman she used to be. The wife, the mother... that woman didn't exist anymore. All that remained was this hollow shell.

Sarah wandered into Joey's room. She hadn't changed a thing in the room since he'd been gone. She and Will had painted the room to look like outer space. They painted moons and stars, different types of planets and rocket ships. He absolutely loved it!

His toys were still scattered all over the floor; Sarah was so careful not to step on any of them. She wouldn't want to break them; Joey would be so upset if his favorite toys were broken.

She lay down on his bed with the rocket ship blanket and matching pillows. It still had his smell. Oh his sweet, sweet smell.

Her head started to swim and anger was rising in her chest. Her beautiful baby boy would never see the third grade. He would never go to high school or the prom. He would never learn to drive a car, or kiss a girl. He would never go to college or fall in love. He would never have a wife and children of his own. How could this happen? How could she be left here to live when the people she loved more than life itself were gone?

Why?

That question burned in her heart day and night. It never went away.

Ever...

Sarah's only family, besides Will and Joey, were her mother and her grandfather. She never knew her father and her mother spent all of Sarah's childhood looking for a good time and a man to take care of her. Needless to say, her grandfather raised her. She called him Poppy and they were as thick as thieves.

After her Poppy died all Sarah had was Will and Joey. She took Poppy's death pretty hard, but her boys kept her strong. As long as she had Will and Joey she didn't need anyone else.

Now they were gone too. She was completely alone.

She lay there in Joey's bed, sleep finally creeping up on her.

She dreamed.

ζ

Sarah looked at the clock again. It was after 11:00pm. They should have been home by now, Will said they were on their way and he didn't say they were stopping anywhere.

She called his cell phone again. It went to voicemail... again.

"Honey, it's me. I'm getting worried so call me back." She hung up and started to pace.

The pacing definitely wasn't helping so she sat on the couch and turned on the TV. She surfed the channels, but had no idea what was on.

The doorbell rang.

Why is he ringing the doorbell? She thought to herself. She jumped off the couch and ran to the door.

As she opened the door she said, "Where have you two...," she stopped mid sentence.

It wasn't Will and Joey.

Two police officers stood in front of Sarah. One of them spoke. "Ma'am, are you Sarah Bradley?" he asked.

"Yes. What's this about officer? Where's my husband and my son?" the realization of the situation hit her with the force of a hurricane. "Oh my God," she said as her eyes widened and her heart jumped into her throat. Panic quickly rose in her chest and her head started to spin.

"We need you to come with us please,"
the second officer said.

"Are they alright? Are they hurt?"

"I'm afraid you'll need to come down to
the hospital ma'am. There's been an accident."
The officers' composure was nothing less than
numbing. How often did they have to deliver
this kind of news to unsuspecting, distraught
family members?

Sarah was completely dumbstruck; she
managed to piece together a complete sentence
and responded, "Let me get my purse."
Somehow Sarah seemed to be operating on
autopilot. The situation could only be described
as surreal. It was as if she was watching herself
in a movie. This couldn't possibly be happening
to her; this had to be happening to someone
else.

CHAPTER 2

Sarah woke up in a sweat, the dream still fresh in her mind. It was the same dream every time she closed her eyes. The memory of that fateful night. The night that now defined her very existence.

Over and over again she dreamed the same dream.

She sat up, still in Joey's room, and lingered at the edge of the bed. *What time is it?* She wondered. It was still dark out, probably two or three in the morning. She never slept through the night anymore unless she took one of the many pills the doctor had given her. He gave her pills to sleep, pills to stay awake, pills to dull the pain, pills to get through the day. But there wasn't a single pill to help her forget. Oh dear God, why can't she just forget?

Sarah managed to find her way to the kitchen and made a cup of tea for herself. Going through the motions made her feel somewhat normal, but the nagging knowledge that nothing would ever be normal again gnawed at the back of her mind.

I can't do this... I'm done, she thought to herself. *I don't want to be here anymore.* She felt like she was in quicksand, sinking deeper and deeper, struggling to get free. The quicksand was over her head now and she saw only one way out.

Sarah headed for the bathroom with her cup of tea. She sat at the edge of the tub and started the water. She walked over to the medicine cabinet and took out every bottle of pills she could find. Sarah lined them all up on the bathroom counter and just stared at them. If she did this there would be no turning back. But Sarah had already reached the point of no return and she couldn't stop herself now.

She opened the first bottle and dumped the pills on the counter. She looked at them for a moment before opening the rest, dumping them all into colorful piles on the cool tile countertop. Sarah scooped up a handful of pills and shoved them in her mouth. She washed them down with her tea and then grabbed another handful and another, until the pills were gone.

Sarah undressed and slid herself into the tub. The pills would overtake her in minutes. Or so she hoped.

She waited for the peace to come.

Her head started to spin and she began to feel sick, but she wouldn't let herself throw up. Sarah closed her eyes and waited, fighting her body's rejection of the pills.

She couldn't turn back now, it was almost over. She would be with her family soon. She would be home again and everything would be alright. Sarah's head was spinning and everything around her was turning black. *Almost there, I'm almost home now.*

"Dear God, please forgive me," she whispered.

Sarah was gone.

ζ

The corridor in the hospital went on forever. Everything seemed to be moving in slow motion. The officers were walking in front of her and looked back every few steps. They went through a pair of double doors that read Emergency Room. *She passed several* occupied beds. Some of them had the drapes closed, but most didn't.

She noticed that the officers had stopped and looked into one of the bed stations. There was a young kid surrounded by a congregation of intently focused doctors and nurses. He couldn't have been more than sixteen or seventeen years old.

There was blood everywhere and the vast assembly of green scrubs and white coats surrounding him was scrambling to keep him alive. They moved with a purpose and nothing but death itself would keep them from their mission.

"This way Mrs. Bradley," said one of the officers as he pulled her along.

They stopped at two beds that were side by side. The same roaring sea of green scrubs and white coats surrounded the beds.

She moved closer.

Will was in one of them; he was unconscious and covered with blood. He was wearing an oxygen mask and had all kinds of IV's running through his arms. She barely recognized him. This man looked nothing like her husband, but he was wearing Will's favorite shirt. It had to be him.

She looked at the bed next to him and saw Joey lying there. He was so peaceful. No one was working on him though; he was just lying there in the bed.

"Why aren't you helping my son?" she asked. "Why aren't you doing anything?" Her voice was rising into a panicked yell.

"Nurse, get her out of here please!" exclaimed one of the doctors.

"No! What's going on? I want to see my son!" Sarah cried.

"Please ma'am, you can't help in here. Come with me please," said one of the nurses as she moved toward Sarah and took her gently by the arm.

"No, please... let me stay. I want to stay with my husband and my son, please!"

"I'll come back for you, I promise," said the nurse.

The two police officers each took Sarah by an arm and moved her away from her family. They dragged her out of the emergency room and into an empty waiting room.

ζ

Sarah opened her eyes and looked around. She was still in her bathroom, but it looked different somehow. It was so dark, and all the color seemed to have drained away. Why was she here? She shouldn't still be here. Did something go wrong? She should be with Will and Joey now. She took all those pills, she remembered that. But why isn't she dead?

Sarah was still in the tub, the water was so cold. She climbed out and grabbed her robe. She put it on over her cold, wet body and walked into her bedroom. Someone was there.

It was her Poppy.

He was sitting in Will's overstuffed armchair. "Hi pumpkin," he said to her and smiled.

"Poppy. I don't understand; why are you here? Am I dead?" She asked.

"Yes baby, you are."

"But why am I still here, in my house? Why is it so dark?" she looked around the room, hoping to find the answers to the questions that now flooded her mind. "What are you doing here? Are you here to take me to Will and Joey?"

"I wish I could pumpkin. Unfortunately I can't, you're a... suicide," he said with hesitation.

"What do you mean?"

"You can't be with your family baby, you're a suicide. Suicides don't go to Heaven." The look on his face was so grave.

"Oh no! What did I do?" All the despair she felt in life had followed her in death. She hadn't escaped her pain, she doomed herself to it. She would be destined to linger in this empty house... forever. The leftover shambles of her life of pain, regret and desperation would be her eternal prison. What had she done?

"I screwed up, didn't I Poppy?" Tears were streaming down her face. The realization of her horrible mistake confirming itself in her voice.

"Suicide is never the answer pumpkin. No matter how much we are suffering it isn't for us to decide the end of our time here." He stood up and walked over to her.

"I'm going to be here forever. In this house... in pain, aren't I?"

He took her two hands and held them in his and said, "No pumpkin. Believe it or not Heavenly Father loves you and doesn't want you to suffer. The gift that he gives us in life he extends to us even in death."

"What do you mean? What gift?" she asked.

"The gift of *free will* of course," he replied with a smile.

"*Free will?* How will that help me?"

"Before you can understand how it will help you, you must first understand that this is not the end. It is only the beginning for you. Death is the beginning of our *eternal life* pumpkin. You have a chance to make it right, to save yourself."

"How?" she asked.

"An angel will come to see you. He will offer you a chance at redemption. But this second chance comes with a price, so you must be ready. If you choose not to go with him, then you will have to stay here in this prison you've created for yourself," he kissed her on her cheek. "I have to go now. The choice is yours; make sure it's the right choice. Will and Joey will be waiting when you are ready. And so will I."

He was gone.

CHAPTER 3

She was so cold and the house was so dark and gloomy. Something was not quite right; it was like the house was withering away. Almost as if the house had died too. If she ever felt alone before, it couldn't compare to the way she felt now. It was like being sucked into a black hole of despair and loneliness.

Sarah wandered around the empty house she thought would now be her prison. How long was eternity? How long had she already been here? Would this *angel* be here soon? She didn't even know how many days had passed. It could have been weeks or even years. But it could have been only hours too, she didn't know for sure. All she was sure of was that the despair she felt in life couldn't compare to what she was feeling right now.

As she wandered around the house she noticed that the pictures of the family seemed distorted and fuzzy. It was like they were taken out of focus. She checked all the pictures, the ones hanging in the hallway, the pictures on her dresser, even the ones on the fridge. It was the same with all of them. She walked past a mirror and saw that even her own reflection was out of focus. What was happening? Sarah's own prison cell was beginning to deteriorate around her.

She slumped down into Will's chair in their bedroom. Her mind was dwelling on her pain as she stewed in her own self-pity. Her self-pity was only outweighed by her self-loathing. If there was a Hell, this must be it.

Sarah sat there for an unknown amount of time before she saw it. A tiny light in the center of the room. It was the size of dime and just floated there. The light grew bigger and became almost blinding, but it didn't hurt her eyes. She couldn't look away; she was completely mesmerized by the light. Just staring at it brought a feeling of complete peace. A peace she hadn't experienced since before the accident.

As the light grew it began to take on a shape. It was the shape of a man.

"Hello Sarah," said the calm, soothing voice of the light. Soon the light began to subside and the shape of the man became much clearer. He was beautiful! His skin was perfect, like those supermodels that are airbrushed on the covers of magazines. His hair was golden blonde and emitted a soft glow. His eyes were crystal blue and were so calming. He was wearing a pure white suit with a pink tie and a long white trench coat that reached the floor. He smiled at her.

"Hi," she replied. "Are you the angel that's coming for me?"

"Yes I am. My name is David."

"You're different than I pictured."

"Did you think I'd be wearing a white gown and have wings?" he asked with a grin.

"I'm not sure what I expected. But I think the pink tie kind of threw me off a little."

"What, you don't like the tie? I like the tie," he said as he looked down at his pink tie and picked it up in his hands. "Pink is the new black you know... or so they say anyway."

"I like the pink." She smiled at him. It was the first smile she could remember having in months. Or was it years?

"Shall we go?" he asked and reached out his right hand to her.

"Go? You mean I don't have to stay here anymore?"

"Only if you want to," he said. "You don't want to stay here, do you?" He looked around the room with a grimace on his face.

"No. I want to see my family, can I see my family?" she asked, hoping the answer would not be what she expected.

"Not yet Sarah, you need to earn it. Are you ready to earn your redemption?" his hand still reaching out to her.

"Yes," she reached out and took his hand.

"Good answer! I was going to have to stay here until you said yes you know. And I didn't really want to hang out here. No offense."

"None taken. I didn't really want to hang out here anymore either," she replied.

"Didn't think so kiddo. Are you ready?"

"Yes," she answered.

"Ok, hold on to me and close your eyes. We're going for a ride." He grinned from ear to ear and held her tight to him. With a cool swirl of a wind and a bright flash of light Sarah could feel herself lift off the floor. Her breath escaped her and she felt completely free from gravity. She opened her eyes, but all she could see was David's smiling face and that same bright, peaceful light surrounding them.

Within a single moment after she had grabbed on to David and felt weightless she began to feel gravity take over again. The light began to subside and she could feel the ground under her feet. She looked up at David and he was still grinning.

"That never gets old!" he exclaimed. "I love traveling here, it's so awesome!"

CHAPTER 4

Sarah stepped away from David and looked at their surroundings. She definitely wasn't in Kansas anymore. It was beautiful! They were in a huge room that looked like the inside of an old English castle. It was made of stone and was at least ten levels high before it reached up to a vaulted ceiling made of stained glass. Each floor above the ground level was encompassed by an intricate stone balcony that overlooked the main hall where they now stood.

There were many open rooms that branched off from this main hall. The other levels mirrored the first floor with their own rooms surrounding the perimeter of the balcony. These rooms were separated with stone columns that joined together into arched openings. Inside each of the rooms was a fireplace, walls full of books and half a dozen brown leather wingback chairs placed around a table in the center. At each of the far ends of the main hall was a pair of double doors made of gold. They were at least twenty feet in height and nearly as wide. They were so beautiful that Sarah believed they had to be the doors to Heaven.

"Wow!" Sarah exclaimed. "What is this place?"

"This is your new home. Well your temporary home, until you decide otherwise."

"It looks like…" she started to say.

"An old castle. Yeah, I know. A very difficult English Duke decided to change the décor, but everyone seemed to like it so we kept it this way."

"I like it too." She gazed around the place in amazement and wasn't quite sure what to do next.

"Good. Some of the others will be here soon, they'll fill you in and help you get acclimated to your new surroundings. They'll explain your assignments to you also," he explained.

"The others? How many more are there?"

"More than I dare to count. First let's get you into something more appropriate. You don't want to hang out in your robe forever do you?" he said. David snapped his fingers and with no more time than a thought takes to manifest she had on different clothes. "Well, that's much better," he said.

Sarah looked down at herself. She was wearing a suit like David's except it was light grey. The tie wasn't pink, it was dark grey and she didn't have on an overcoat like his either.

"Is this standard *angel* issue?" she asked with a touch of sarcasm.

"Oh no kiddo, that's not *angel* issue attire. You're not ready for that, what you're wearing is standard *soldier* issue." He hadn't caught her sarcasm and had answered her with a completely serious tone.

"*Soldier!* Wait a minute, I'm no *soldier*. I can't even take care of myself, I'm pathetic! Oh no, there's some kind of mistake," she was panicking now.

"There's no mistake Sarah," the voice came from behind David. A tall man with jet black hair and bright green eyes walked around David and started toward Sarah. He had come from out of nowhere.

He was wearing a suit identical to Sarah's except he had on a dark grey floor length trench just like David's. Three more people appeared from behind David, one man and two women. The other man was short and

30

stout with grey hair that was slicked back; he also had on a trench coat.

The two women came into her view; one of them was quite a bit older. She had silver, white hair and a kind face. The other was very young, maybe in her early twenties at the most, but looked as though she had a very rough life while she was alive. She barely made eye contact with Sarah. They didn't have trench coats, just the grey suits like hers.

"Hi Sarah, I'm Nigel," the tall man with the black hair introduced himself and walked over to her. "This here is Vinchetto," he looked at the short, stout man and motioned to him.

"How ya doin'?" Vinchetto said to her. He had an incredibly thick New York accent. When he got closer Sarah noticed that his suit had pin stripes. His name, his accent and his suit screamed out *mob*. "You can call me by my nickname."

"Let me guess, your nickname is *Vinnie*, right?" Sarah said.

"Actually it's *Vinnie the Bull*, if you want to get technical about it."

"Ok... can I just call you Vinchetto?" Sarah replied.

"You can call me whatever you want sweetheart," he replied with a smile and then he kissed the back of her hand. Sarah giggled like a little kid.

"Moving right along. This here is Maggie," the older woman with the silver, white hair nodded at Sarah. "And this is Calista," Nigel looked over at the younger woman. She looked at Sarah but quickly looked away. Calista moved away from the group and walked into one of the rooms.

"Alright then... I guess I'll be going now. Sarah, make yourself at home. Ask Nigel any questions you may have and I'm sure they'll all give you the rundown of your new life here," said David. "Good luck. I'll be back to check on you."

"Wait! What is this place?" she asked.

"This is purgatory kid," he answered her as if he was pointing out the insanely obvious.

"Hey David," Vinchetto called out. "Nice tie. Pink today, huh?"

"What's with the hostility toward the tie? I like this tie, what's wrong with...," he trailed off and then as quickly as they had appeared, he vanished.

"We like to call this place *Salvation City*. Kinda fits don't it?" said Vinchetto.

CHAPTER 5

Purgatory, Limbo, the Spiritual World. Almost every religion or belief has a term for the place that Sarah Bradley now called *home*. She just never expected it to be an actual, tangible place filled with other lost souls just like her. Yet here she was, not in Heaven, but not in Hell either.

Any questions she may have had about what really happens when you die had been washed away with the force of a tidal wave. Faith had now become truth. This place, though only a waiting room of sorts, was more beautiful than anything she'd ever seen during her life on earth. She was in complete and total awe.

"Hey kid, come on in here with us," Vinchetto said to her as he headed for the room that Calista had disappeared into earlier. Sarah followed them and they sat in the big wingback chairs by the oversized fireplace. The fire crackled, but didn't put off any heat. Nigel leaned on the bookcase next to the fireplace and just watched her.

"So Sarah, I suppose you have a lot of questions about who we are and what we do," Nigel said to her.

"Yes. I'm not sure why I'm here. Well, I know *why* I'm here, but I don't know what I'm supposed to do," she said. "What is it you do exactly?"

Maggie laughed with a smoker's rasp and said, "Go ahead Nigel, tell her. And make sure you don't sugar coat it either."

Nigel looked at Maggie and then looked around the room at the rest of this motley crew of redeeming souls. "We save people that are in despair. We try to keep them from killing themselves or killing others," he paused a moment and then continued. "Well, that's the plan anyway. Obviously we don't always succeed."

"You mean people like me?" Sarah asked. Calista looked up at her and then looked at Vinchetto.

"Yeah, but not just the people that want to *off* themselves," explained Vinchetto. "We get called to all kinds of situations. People aren't very good to each other, but sometimes we can prevent bad things from happening.

You know, keep them from hurting or killing each other."

"How do you know when something *bad* is happening or going to happen?"

Maggie answered this question, "That's where Leo comes in. He's our *Proctor*, the head of the *Redemption Angels*. He's in charge of all of us and gives us our assignments."

"How many of us are there?" asked Sarah.

"None of *us* know for sure. Hundreds, thousands, could even be millions. Leo knows, David probably knows too. And of course Heavenly Father knows," replied Nigel.

"Wow, I would have never thought there were so many sad and lonely people roaming around in the world," Sarah's eyes just glazed over as she pondered the revelation that she wasn't alone in the world after all.

"Not all of them killed themselves. Some are here for other reasons," explained Vinchetto. "Maybe they did something really bad or even unforgivable in the eyes of everyone... except God."

"Why are you here?" Sarah asked Vinchetto.

He chuckled, "Well, I wasn't a very good person when I was alive. I hurt a lot of people, even killed some people. And I did it for the worst reason of all."

"What reason is that?" Sarah asked with a look on her face that revealed a child-like curiosity.

"Because I could," he paused for a moment nodding his head, "Yeah... because I could. I thought I was *all powerful* and in control of everything. I wanted people to respect me, *Vinnie the Bull!*"

"Did they?"

"No. Mostly they just feared me. My family feared me too, that was the worst part." He turned away from her with shame on his face and stared into the fire.

"So," said Sarah changing the subject, "how do we *save* these people from themselves?"

"Now that's where it gets tricky. We're not the only ones fighting for these people's souls," said Nigel. "We try to beat them there, but we're not always the first on the scene when someone is in a bad situation. Satan sends his own *soldiers* to help these lost souls succeed in whatever misdeeds they're up to."

"You mean like *demons* or something?" Sarah asked with a hint of disbelief.

"Or *something* alright," said Calista. It was the first time she had spoken since their arrival.

"Not just demons. He sends all kinds of nasty vermin to keep us from saving these people," said Maggie. "We're usually outnumbered three to one when we're battling for someone's soul."

"How do you ever win when you're so outnumbered?"

"Because we are, and always will be, stronger," said Nigel. "No matter how hard Satan tries to stain the hearts and minds of mankind, people will always have an unfaltering desire to survive and do right. They don't always realize it until that exact moment of truth is upon them though. And sometimes they don't realize it until it's too late, but usually we prevail."

Vinchetto spoke up, "Things have been changing though. Satan's been getting stronger, people have been falling into despair much easier and they've been hurting and killing each other a lot more these days," he looked over at Nigel. "We haven't been able to save the numbers of souls that we used to."

"He's right, things are changing in the world. Greed, fear, hatred, all these things have been escalading for decades and it's been getting harder to beat back the demons." Nigel continued. "The timeless battle between good and evil over the souls of mankind has been kicked up a notch and we have to be ready to do whatever it takes to win."

"Ok. What do I do?" Sarah asked as she looked around the room at the others.

Maggie wheezed out a laugh and Vinchetto said, "Well all right then, let's get you geared up."

"Geared up?" Sarah wasn't quite sure what he meant by that, but she was sure she would soon find out.

CHAPTER 6

Vinchetto led her into another room off the main hall and the others all followed. Either Sarah hadn't noticed before, or they had all just arrived, but the place was now buzzing with people. Every one of them was dressed like her. More *angels of redemption*.

Some of them took notice of Sarah and smiled or nodded at her, but most just hurried about from room to room talking with others or even floating from one floor to the next. There had to be hundreds of them, maybe thousands, and they seemed to congregate in groups. Just like Nigel's group they all seemed to form some kind of a team.

There were people from all walks of life. They even appeared to be from different time periods since this place was eternal, it would make sense that there were souls here for decades or even centuries.

The room that they were in now seemed to be some sort of weapons room. The walls were covered with all types of swords, daggers, guns, crossbows, shields, the choices were endless. She could never have imagined anything like this in real life. There were long tables that stood in the middle of the room that were covered with more weapons. She felt like she had just stepped into a modern day vampire movie, *Dracula meets Gabriel*. It was unbelievable, what was she supposed to do with all this? She had never even held a gun, let alone fire one.

"Let's get you loaded up," said Vinchetto.

"I'm sorry, what?" Sarah replied in disbelief.

Nigel stepped over to her, "We'll get you started with something simple." He reached up on one of the walls and took down two swords. They were each only about a foot and a half in length and identical in every detail. It was obvious that they were meant to be used as a pair.

"Here, try these. They're not too long and you should be able to handle them alright." He tucked them under her belt, one on each hip.

She crossed her arms and grabbed them by the handles and pulled them out of their sheaths. She was amazed at the ease in which she was able to handle the swords. Sarah held them with the back of the blades flush to her forearms, the way an assassin would hold a knife. It was almost as if she had used them before, they felt so comfortable in her hands. She swung them around in a figure eight and twirled them like they were batons; she then slipped them back into their sheaths.

"Nice! I think those will do just fine. For now anyway," Nigel said with a satisfied grin on his face.

"Looks like someone's a natural," said Maggie.

"Let's hope so," said Calista. She didn't seem to like the idea of Sarah jumping right into combat. Sarah wasn't sure if Calista was worried about her or just didn't like her very much. Time would tell, but Sarah couldn't worry about being in a popularity contest right now. Everything she had ever known had completely changed. Life as she had known it was gone forever. It all seemed like a distant memory now, the only thing that remained was Will and Joey and her love for them. Everything else she had left behind just didn't matter.

ζ

"Hello everyone," came a deep voice from the main hall. People from all over wandered in to meet the voice. In the middle of the room was a huge hologram of a man in a solid white suit. He was quite old, and had pure white hair and a matching beard. His eyes were a piercing blue just like David's.

He spoke again, "Nigel, I have an assignment for you and your team. This one is a tough one so I'm sending in Natalia and her team too."

"What's the skinny on this one Leo?" asked the voice of a woman behind Nigel and his crew. She had a suit that matched Nigel's all the way down to the trench coat. She was tall and lean and had curly red hair as bright as the sun. It was so long it reached her waist and she kept it pulled away from her beautiful face.

She continued, "You never send anyone in with Nigel, this must be a doozy," she looked over at Nigel and winked, he smiled at her.

"It is a *doozy*... as you put it Natalia. We have a quadruple murder and suicide on this one," his voice was so stoic. He had been at his job for centuries, or maybe longer and nothing seemed to ruffle his feathers.

"Is this a family Leo, or some kind of crime gone wrong?" asked Nigel.

"A husband and father. He lost his job, he's been drinking endlessly and he just received news from his wife that she's leaving him and taking the kids with her." He paused for a moment and then looked directly at Nigel, "This is Sarah's first assignment and I want you and Vinchetto to keep her close. There's a *higher level* demon on this one and it's Vinchetto's old nemesis."

"*Arzulu?* You don't need to worry about me Leo, I can handle that piece of trash," replied Vinchetto.

"I'm not worried about *you*; my concern is the *lower level* demons and the *soldiers* he brings with him. Bring Sarah up to speed before you take her into the lion's den. He'll have some heavy re-enforcements with him."

"Who are the victims Leo?" asked a man from Natalia's group.

"The husband's name is Michael Grayson, age thirty-six and the wife is Debbie Grayson, age thirty-four. There are two kids, little Mikey, age four and Suzy is ten months." He continued, "The fourth victim is Debbie's sister, Kara Wilkins. She is picking up the family so they can stay with her. She arrives before Michael takes his own life and he kills her too. She has a husband and three kids," Leo paused briefly. "I know I don't have to tell you how important it is that she *does not* get to that house before Michael completes his task."

He stopped and then looked around at everyone, his stoic look melting and emotion revealing itself in his piercing blue eyes. "If you can't stop Michael it is *imperative* that Kara does not make it to the house before he kills himself."

Nigel and Natalia looked at each other; they knew exactly what needed to be done.

"Ok Leo, show us the family," said Natalia.

Leo disappeared from the hologram and a scene began to fast forward like an old home movie. It stopped on a scene with a man pacing a bedroom, yelling and waving a gun recklessly in his hand. A woman sat on the bed holding a baby and a small child cowered behind her. They were all crying and the woman was begging the man to put the gun down so they could talk.

The home movie began to fast forward again and stopped at the Wilkins' home. Kara was laughing and joking with her kids and her husband. This scene was filled with happiness and love, a far cry from the previous scene they had just witnessed. The picture was gone and Leo was back.

"Get to work *angels*, I'll be watching," said Leo and then he faded away.

Chapter 7

"Let's move like we got a purpose people!" yelled Vinchetto. Everyone hurried into the weapons room and suited up like a well trained military unit. After everyone had geared up they filed out in perfect formation into the center of the main hall, and in the blink of an eye they were transported to their destination. With a flash of light they disappeared one by one.

"Let's go Sarah. Stick with me and Calista and you'll be fine," Maggie grabbed her arm and pulled her toward the main hall. Nigel and Natalia were the first to go, there were only a few angels remaining.

Maggie took her right arm and Calista took her left arm, "Hold on Sarah, here we go!" yelled Calista. With a flash of brilliant light and a rush of wind they were weightless and they were off.

ζ

Only moments after they left the comfort and security of *Salvation City* they arrived into a scenario that can only be described as complete and total chaos. The air reeked of sulfur, much like the stench of rotting eggs, and there was a feeling of complete dread and anxiety in the room.

The atmosphere itself was hazy and dim as if all the light in the room was being drawn out by some unseen force. The foul, rotting carcasses of the Devil's *crows* were perched on nearly every surface in the room. The *crows* looked as though they had been dead for months and their eyes were a pus-like yellow in color. They cawed and scratched and flew around the room causing as much fear and unrest as they could, as if their mere presence could suck the life force out of anything.

The *crows* weren't the only horrid creatures that were flying around the room. There were at least a half a dozen beasts about the size of a small child, but looked like a cross between a pterodactyl and a devil from some cheesy costume shop. They were completely hairless and had warty, grey skin. In the place where their ears should have been were grotesque spiky bumps resembling horns, and their eyes were blood red with black slits for pupils. They had no noses, only snake-like slits.

But it was their teeth that scared Sarah the most. They were all different lengths and pointed to razor sharpness, like those of some kind of mutated vampires. They screeched as they darted through the air. It was the most maddening sound Sarah had ever heard in her life. For a moment she believed she might actually go mad.

She ducked as one of the vile beasts swooped toward her. Calista shoved her out of the way and she fell headlong onto the bed. Calista raised up the crossbow she had in her hands and started firing at the foul creatures. She hit one that passed in front of her and it quickly burst into black smoke, and then dissipated into a fine grey dust. She hit two more and they reaped the same fate as the first.

Maggie drew two handguns and joined one of Natalia's team members and started shooting the decaying *crows*.

"Thanks Maggie," hollered Samuel.

"Any time my friend," replied Maggie.

"Maggie, watch out!" cried Calista. Behind Maggie one of the flying *soldier beasts* veered toward her head, trying to take it clean off. Maggie hit the floor and Samuel blasted it with a shotgun.

Sarah was completely overwhelmed by the scene that was playing out in front of her. She had never in her wildest imagination believed that anything in this room could ever be real. Yet here she was, right in the middle of an honest to goodness battle between *angles* and *demons*.

"Sarah, cover the *innocents!*" yelled Calista. Sarah looked behind her and realized that Debbie Grayson, little Mikey and baby Suzy were huddled together at the head of the bed terrified out of their minds. Sarah jumped across the bed and put her arms around the horrified family.

"Talk to them Sarah, tell them everything will be alright. Tell them that God loves them. Do it Sarah!" screamed Maggie, her voice barely audible over the violent screeching from the flying beasts.

"Shhhh! Don't be afraid little ones. We are here, we will protect you." Sarah continued her reassuring words over and over again. Mikey and Suzy looked directly into her eyes. Their hysterical cries stopped and they focused only on Sarah's face. Sarah stroked Debbie's shoulders and then her face, repeating her words of comfort.

It was then that Sarah had time to really take a good look at the scene that was unfolding in the room around her. Nigel was fighting toe to toe with the most terrifying being she has ever seen. He was taller than Nigel and looked *almost* like a man, but was still very different. His face was the color of ash and he had the same razor sharp, jagged array of teeth as the *soldier demons* that were flying around the room. His lifeless eyes were solid black and his fingernails were long and torn and stained a sick yellowish, brown color. His cheek bones were completely sunken in and his black lips were cracked and oozing some sort of thick, black blood.

The clash of swords between Nigel and the demon was deafening. They moved so quickly, thrusting their swords at each other. Nigel swung his sword in a swift motion across the demons belly. Black blood sprayed out everywhere.

"Is that all you have old man? It will take more than that to send me back to Hell," taunted the demon. Nigel showed no emotion and kept up his vigilant fight. Again they continued to clash swords, pushing each other back and forth across the room.

"You know you won't win Barthalius! Why even bother?" stated Nigel in a casual tone.

"If you think this is all my *Master* will send then you had better think again," claimed the demon as he let out the most horrifying cackle.

Vinchetto was side by side with Michael Grayson, talking to him and telling him how worthy he is, how much he is loved, and that everything would work out. He continued on and on, calming Michael and soothing him. He gently rubbed his shoulders and put his hands on his head as he talked to him.

"Michael, put down the gun, you don't need it. Your family loves you and needs you. You don't want to hurt them, you love them and they love you," whispered Vinchetto into Michael Grayson's ears.

"No, no, no!" yelled Michael. "You don't love me! You want to leave me… you're going to leave me and take away my kids! I'm not going to let you do that Debbie!"

"Michael, please! Don't do this, let the kids go watch cartoons in the other room and we'll talk. Just me and you... please Michael!" begged Debbie as tears poured from her eyes.

Vinchetto didn't give up, he kept talking to Michael. Soothing him. The chaos in the room was getting worse. He could see the others battling the *soldiers*, but they just kept coming. For every *soldier* or *crow* that was killed another appeared to replace it. The *higher level* demon needed to be taken out or they would be fighting in quicksand all night.

"Vinchetto... I was hoping to see you tonight," said a voice from behind him.

"Arzulu, I wondered when you would show up," replied Vinchetto as he slowly turned to face the demon that addressed him.

"You don't seem surprised to see me. Damn that *Proctor* of yours! He always spoils the surprise!" Arzulu laughed and drew his sword.

"Let's do this!" yelled Vinchetto and lunged for the demon.

CHAPTER 8

Natalia and three others from her team were in the Wilkins' house. Their only mission was to stop Kara from going to the Grayson's house before Nigel's team could accomplish their mission. Sometimes this was much harder than battling demons.

"Honey, before you go to your sister's can you help me in here a minute?" yelled Kara's husband Dan from the other room.

"Oh for the love of Pete, what does that man want now?" she mumbled to herself. Natalia followed her from room to room as she scurried about picking up messes here and there, whispering to her. She told Kara not to go, for her to wait awhile. She told her that she was needed here and there was no need to rush off to her sister's house just yet.

When the situation was dire an angel could manipulate objects in the physical world. Depending on the strength of the angel this task could be easy or extremely difficult.

Fortunately Natalia has been at this for many, many decades. She was a pro at manipulating just about anything she wanted in the physical world.

Natalia walked over to the kitchen table and knocked one of the kids' glasses of milk onto the floor. The glass shattered and there was milk and broken glass everywhere. Kara jumped at the sudden sound of breaking glass and abruptly turned around to find the source, her heart pounding in her chest. She stared at the mess on the floor and then at the table. *How in the hell did that fall off the table?* She thought to herself. The kids were in the family room, it couldn't have been them. *Weird... oh well.*

Kara's *mom autopilot* took control of her and she began the dreary task of cleaning up. As she was bent over a puddle of milk and broken glass her husband Dan yelled out to her again. "Honey! It's really important, can you come in here? Just real quick, I promise," he hollered.

Boy, Joshua is good, thought Natalia. Joshua from her team was in with Kara's husband, and Sophie and Hannah were with the kids. She had sent Samuel with Nigel's team.

"That man is going to drive me to drink," Kara said to herself. "Just a minute for crying out loud!" she yelled back.

It didn't take her long to clean up the milk and broken glass, she was a professional *mess-picker-upper*. With three kids she'd have to be. She headed down the hallway and into the master bedroom where Dan was calling to her incessantly. He was lying on the bed wearing only his robe and smiled at her with a menacing, little boy grin.

"Hey baby, what's your sign?" he asked her playfully.

"Closed!" she replied and then jumped on the bed next to him. "What do you want?" she asked with a smile.

"What do I want... well let me think about that for a minute."

"Seriously Dan, the kids are in the other room. They'll hear us," said Kara.

"They're busy watching a movie," he had an answer for anything she could throw at him. "Come on, I'll be quick."

"Isn't that the story of my life," Kara laughed. "You know I have to pick up Debbie and the kids."

"I know; that's why I want some now. Lord knows when I'll get any after they're here."

"Ha ha!" she slapped him playfully on the arm. "Alright, you've worn me down you smooth talker."

"Woo Hoo!"

"But don't make it too quick, I want it to last longer than it takes me to get undressed. Otherwise it's just not worth it." Kara jumped up and closed the bedroom door.

Natalia and Joshua looked at each other and did a *high five*. They left the bedroom and joined Sophie and Hannah in the family room with the kids.

"Great job Joshua," complimented Natalia.

"Well, you know... what can I say? I'm good." He huffed his breath on his fingernails and buffed them on his suit in an effort to brag about his skills. They all just watched him and rolled their eyes. He's so young and full of himself that they couldn't help but love him.

"Sophie, I need you to check on Nigel's progress. If he's not ready we'll need to make sure that we keep Kara here," said Natalia. "She'll only be occupied for a little while and we don't know what they're up against over there."

"I'm on it," said Sophie and with a flash she transported herself to the Grayson's house.

CHAPTER 9

Sophie knew there would be an ugly scene at the Grayson house, but she wasn't prepared for this much chaos. There were twice as many *soldiers* as she expected and both Nigel and Vinchetto were battling *higher level* demons. She'd seen her share of *crows* in her time, but never this many in one place. The room was so filled with the evil creatures that they almost completely blocked out all the light. The room was dark enough already without their help.

She could see Samuel and Maggie shooting the *crows*, but Calista was waging an all out war with the *soldier beasts* that were flying around the room. She quickly joined Calista in her battle against the grotesque monsters.

Sarah had drawn her swords and was slicing at the *soldiers* as they dove, talons drawn and teeth bared, at her and the family.

She had slayed quite a few, but they just kept coming.

Arzulu and Vinchetto had been fighting over Michael, their words clashing as much as their swords. For every word of love and encouragement from Vinchetto, Arzulu did his best to outdo him with hate and degradation.

"Michael, you're useless! No one needs you, no one wants you!" Arzulu's words sliced through the room like a razor, boring onto Michael's mind. "Do it! Kill them, kill them all!"

Vinchetto brought his sword through the air and sliced it across the demon's face. His rotted, black blood sprayed everywhere.

Vinchetto cried out to Michael, "Don't do it Michael, you love your family and they love you. You don't need to do this, there is a way out. Trust in your faith!"

"No!" yelled Arzulu, black spittle flew from his dead lips. "There is no way out, it's over for you. End it now!"

Michael stumbled around confused and feeling sick. He grabbed at his head, the gun still gripped in his hand.

"Debbie, I can't let you leave. You won't take my family away from me!" Michael raised the gun and moved closer to his terrified wife.

"No Michael, please! Don't do this," begged Debbie.

"It's too late!" cried Michael.

"Vinchetto!" yelled Sarah. "Stop him!"

Vinchetto knew time had run out. He yelled out to this *army of angels* and said, "Someone take this wretched demon!" Samuel and Maggie answered his call and quickly swarmed Arzulu, overtaking him long enough for Vinchetto to get away. Vinchetto jumped in front of Michael just as he squeezed the trigger on the gun. The bullet fired out of the barrel in slow motion and Vinchetto's coat opened up into the most beautiful pair of dark grey wings. Sarah watched in awe as the bullet hit Vinchetto's wings and disappeared into nothing, lost forever to its intended target.

Michael stood motionless and watched this miracle unfold, only then realizing what he had just done. He dropped to his knees and cried uncontrollably. The gun fell from his hand and Debbie quickly jumped up and kicked it under the bed. She dropped to her knees, baby Suzy still in her arms, and cried with her husband.

"I'm so sorry! What have I done?" cried Michael.

"It's alright now, it's over," replied Debbie, not yet realizing the magnitude of the situation. That reflection would come later when the dust settled. Little Mikey joined them on the floor and everyone cried together.

"NO!" yelled Arzulu and Barthalius in unison. They had lost this battle, but there would be others. Their *soldier demons* and *crows* began to burst into black smoke and disappeared into dust. One by one they were gone and with a violent tornado of black smoke and flames Arzulu and Barthalius vanished with their fellow soldiers of *Satan's army*.

ζ

Nigel looked around the room at everyone. This battle was tough, but he's been in worse. His main concern, however, was for Sarah.

Samuel and Sophie looked at each other and chuckled. They knew that Natalia would be disappointed she missed this raging war. She loved this stuff!

"How is everyone?" asked Nigel. "Sarah, how are you holding up?"

"That was awesome!" she exclaimed. "I've never been so terrified and so excited all at the same time! Are all the battles like this?"

"Lord help us, I hope not," replied Calista, she liked the easier assignments.

"That was a rush wasn't it?" asked Vinchetto.

"Vinchetto, I've never seen anything more amazing than what I saw you do. Now I can see why they call you *Vinnie the Bull*," said Sarah. "And I didn't know you had wings!" She was completely awestruck.

Nigel chuckled, "That's what our coats are. They're wings. Pretty cool, huh?"

"How do I get a pair?" Sarah asked.

"You have to earn them," answered Samuel. He and Sophie didn't have any either, Natalia was the only one in their group with wings.

"Samuel, Sophie," said Nigel. "Go and tell Natalia that it's over, mission accomplished."

"On our way," replied Samuel.

"Hey guys," said Vinchetto. "Thanks. Really."

"Anytime *Vinnie the Bull*," replied Sophie with a wink and a smile. With a flash of light they headed to Natalia's location.

"Ok *angels*, let's go home," said Nigel.

One by one with a brilliant flash of light they transported back to *Salvation City*. Calista looped her arm in Sarah's and they went home together. Soon Sarah would learn to transport herself, but for now she liked the company.

CHAPTER 10

Back in the safety and comfort of *Salvation City* they sat together in one of the rooms and reflected on the events of their mission. They were joined by Natalia and her group as they shared their account of the Wilkins' household during the chaos that had been unleashed at the Grayson's home. There was quite a contrast between the current lives of the two sisters, but if anything is certain in life it's how quickly the tides can shift. Tomorrow may hold a different fate for both families.

Satan had sent two of his *higher level* demons to manipulate the situation. This of course wasn't unheard of, but not likely with the small number of *innocents* involved. One *higher level* should have been sufficient in this particular case.

Normally Satan would only send out more than one of his *higher levels* for serial killers, mass suicides and collection purposes at the scene of natural disasters, freak accidents, freeway pile-ups and so forth. But lately Nigel noticed that the number of demons that were sent was almost overkill, even for the Prince of Darkness and his flair for the dramatic.

Something is going on in the world and Satan was doing everything in his power to claim his prize. Times were clearly changing and Satan's business was constantly expanding to keep up with that change.

His business, of course, consisted of soul collecting, recruiting, feeding the misery and pain of people for his own agenda and adding fuel to the fire in the minds of the depraved. Just to name a few. He was a master manipulator who thrived on the suffering of the weak and the desperate. And needless to say, business was booming.

Leo clearly must have known this, that's why he sent in two teams. Nigel was in one of the other rooms off the main hall reporting to Leo on their latest success.

"Nigel, that was a close call today, but I want to tell you what a great job all of you did. You saved everyone... including Michael."

"Thanks Leo, my team's the best and Vinchetto was at the top of his game, as always."

"He does have quite an unorthodox way about him. But I must admit he's one of the best... Next to you and Natalia of course," said Leo.

"Sarah did really well for her first time out," said Nigel. "It was pretty rough in there and she was completely composed and focused the whole time. I know when she's ready she'll want to go home, but I hope she'll consider staying on with us. We could use her."

"Is that the only reason you want her to stay?"

"What do you mean?" asked Nigel.

"She has an uncanny resemblance to your Molly," said Leo, as if he was stating the obvious.

"Yeah... I noticed," replied Nigel. "But that has no bearing on anything; you should know me by now. I would never keep anyone from their calling, no matter what I think they should do. Or what I want for that matter."

"I know, I never doubt any of your motives. It was just an observation."

"Duly noted," Nigel continued. "Any assignments coming up soon for Sarah?"

"Actually, one for Maggie. But I want her to take Sarah."

"Is it an easy one?" asked Nigel.

"A *jumper*," said Leo. "A forty-five year old man in Las Vegas named Steven Carvell. He's a hotel executive and he's recently been through and very nasty divorce. His wife took everything, including the kids."

"Ouch!" replied Nigel.

"That's just the tip of the iceberg. He's about to receive news that he's under investigation for embezzlement and he'll be fired shortly thereafter," said Leo.

Nigel waited for Leo to continue.

"He has a rooftop key for the hotel where he works. It's a forty story fall, not very pleasant. I hate the *jumper* assignments. *Innocents* don't get over those easily... if ever."

"There's no turning back for a *jumper*. You think Maggie and Sarah can handle it alone?"

"Send Vinchetto with them, this guy hasn't been living the good life and there could be some resistance when they get there. Besides, I think he'll like visiting some of his old stomping grounds." Leo smiled at the thought of Vinchetto's old lifestyle and said, "*What happens in Vegas stays in Vegas.*"

"I'll feel better if he goes with them anyway. There's been heavy demon activity at *all* the assignments lately, not just the big ones," Nigel was feeling reassured at the thought of Vinchetto watching over Sarah.

"Oh, one more thing, the *Angels of War* will be replenishing their troops so you'll see them marching through *Salvation City* soon."

The *Angels of War* were an elite unit of specialized angels whose sole purpose was to accompany every human soldier on every battlefield at all times. It was a tough assignment and only the truly worthy were called for this duty. It was quite an honor to be called as an *Angel of War*; many angels strove for this honor for decades or even centuries. But it also took the greatest of sacrifices.

There was nothing more destructive to mankind than the devastation of war. And even more destructive were the demons that were unleashed during these ultimate human conflicts. Although they were bound by the same rules as every other demon, there was no way to stop all the atrocities committed by the scourge of Hell. The *Angels of War* had to keep them at bay the best they could while they comforted the souls in despair during and after wars had been waged. Their task was immense, but no one was more up to the challenge than these self-sacrificing warriors.

"I always love to see them march through here. They're so inspiring to all of us."

"Still thinking about joining the *Angels of War?*" Leo asked Nigel.

Nigel replied after a thoughtful pause, "I'm not ready yet. I have a long way to go before I'm worthy to walk along side them."

"You're closer than you think," said Leo and his hologram face faded. Nigel was left in the room alone to reflect on his last statement. He wasn't sure if we wanted to leave this ragtag team of lost souls just yet, even if he was worthy enough to be an *Angel of War.*

"Hey Nigel," Vinchetto yelled to him from across the main hall.

Nigel snapped out of his trance and looked up at his fellow warrior, his comrade in arms, his friend. He smiled at him and replied, "Yeah Vinchetto, I'll be right there." He joined the others and took a few moments to enjoy their company and their friendship as they laughed and joked with each other. He was truly lucky to be in the company of such honorable fellow souls sharing the same mission to redeem themselves in the eyes of their Heavenly Father. There was no place he would rather be right now... at this very moment.

CHAPTER 11

"Sarah, come with me. I'm taking you on a tour of *Salvation City*," said Vinchetto.

"Alright," smiled Sarah.

"Take my arm," he said and held out his right arm, elbow pointed out. She looped her arm in his and they lifted off the ground, rising to the second floor. They floated to the balcony and landed softly onto the walkway that surrounded the opening below. There were other angels that were traveling around in the same fashion, floating from floor to floor. It was all so graceful.

The rooms that encompassed the balcony were designed and set up the same as the ground floor. They were filled with other angels deep in conversation or bustling about the walkway.

"Hey there Vinchetto, who's the new recruit?" asked someone that was walking towards them.

"Hey Brad, this here is Sarah," replied Vinchetto.

"Hi Sarah, welcome to *Salvation City.*"

"Thanks. It's nice to meet you," answered Sarah.

"I'm sure all of this is a little overwhelming, huh?" said Brad.

"Just a little," she replied.

"Well, hang in there. You'll be fine," Brad smiled at her as he hitched his thumb toward Vinchetto. "If you ever decide to dump this guy and join up with a real crew of guardians let me know, we're always looking for talented help."

"I'll keep that in mind," Sarah smiled and looked at Vinchetto.

"Ok Brad, recruiting time is over. Beat it!" Vinchetto laughed.

"Yeah, yeah. Nice to meet you Sarah," Brad reached out to shake Sarah's hand. "I'm sure we'll see each other around."

"I'm sure we will," replied Sarah with a smile as she shook his hand. Brad continued on his way and caught up with some of his group and the conversation was buzzing. About Sarah no doubt. She turned around and saw that Brad and the others were watching her and Vinchetto as they continued on their way.

"Come on, I'm taking you to the training room," he held out his arm for Sarah to take. They lifted off again, but this time they went all the way to the top floor. It was the only floor that was different from all the rest.

The entire floor was one completely open room that encircled the opening overlooking the main hall below. Weapons lined the walls all around the entire floor and people were sparring everywhere. Some used swords and knives and some had bows and arrows. Others were firing away at targets using guns from just about every time era. A few warriors were actually fighting in hand-to-hand combat. It was quite a sight to behold.

"There's an area open over there," Vinchetto led her to an open spot and walked over to the weapons wall. He took down the swords that Sarah had used in her first assignment and he chose a long Katana sword to spar with.

"Are we going to sword fight?" she asked.

"Well, not like pirates or anything, but yeah. I want you to get used to your weapons in case you're ever up against a *higher level.*"

"Ok, I guess I'm ready," she held her swords, one in each hand standing in an attack stance. They started sparring, easy at first, but growing more aggressive as Sarah became more comfortable with her weapons. As she grew more confident in her skills her motions became faster and more fluid. She was getting the hang of this, and quite quickly. Vinchetto was impressed.

"So, *Vinnie the Bull*, I know your story, but tell me about the others," said Sarah.

"Well, Maggie was a suicide. She was alone, buried in financial problems and just couldn't see any other way out."

"How'd she do it?"

"Razor blades to the wrist. You talk about doing it the hard way."

"Ouch! How long has she been here?" Sarah asked.

"Oh, by *mortal* time I'd say about twenty-five years."

"That's a long time! Am I going to be here that long?"

"That all depends on you. Everyone receives their redemption in their own time. Maggie's time hasn't come yet, when she's ready she'll know," replied Vinchetto.

"Is that why some angels have wings and some don't?" she asked.

"Yeah, when you've earned your redemption you'll get your wings *or* be allowed to cross over into Heaven."

"Why are you still here? You've earned your *redemption*."

"Yeah, but I really like what I do. I was a really bad guy when I was alive and this is my chance to make it right. You know what I mean?" he asked.

"Actually I think I do. So, we get a choice even here?"

"Of course! We always get a choice, that's *His* gift to us... always," he stated as they continued with their sparring.

"Ok, how about Nigel?"

"He's been here since the late 1700's. He's one of the oldest of the *angels of redemption*, almost 250 years by my count."

"Wow! Was he a suicide too?" she asked him.

"No, he lost his family to the plague. They were on their way to the *new America*, but he was the only one to make it. He lost his wife, Molly, and his two little girls," he continued. "After that he lost his mind. When he reached America he went crazy and killed some people, they hanged him in the village square and the rest is history."

"What about Calista?"

He stopped sparring with her and paused for a moment. "She overdosed on drugs. She was really young, but her life was hard and she made some really bad choices. So, like the rest of us, she wound up here."

"I don't think she likes me very much," Sarah confided to Vinchetto.

"Actually just the opposite. She feels responsible for you," he was hesitant to tell her, he felt as though he was betraying Calista's confidence. "Me and her were there when you killed yourself," he confessed.

Now Sarah understood Calista's reluctance to talk to her. She knew that Calista had to be in pain over this, but she didn't know if there was anything she could say to put her heart at ease. Calista was so young and she was carrying around such a heavy burden of guilt.

"Well, that explains a lot," was all she could say at this moment. Then she added, "It wasn't her fault you know, I didn't want to be there anymore."

"Yeah, but it's still hard to lose one of your *mortals*. I made sure that you were assigned to our team. That way we could watch over you until you earned your redemption."

"I can't think of any other angels that I'd rather hang out with than you guys." Then she added, "Until I get to go home, anyway."

"Fair enough," he smiled and they continued with their sparring.

CHAPTER 12

Jason Stevens wheeled himself into his bedroom. Ever since the car accident he's been confined to a wheelchair and has become a huge burden on his parents. The doctors told him the damage wouldn't be permanent and he would be able to walk again with a few dozen surgeries and a whole lot of therapy. But the financial ramifications would be astronomical and he couldn't justify putting his parents through more than he already had.

They took care of his every need financially, physically and emotionally. They'd been through enough doctor visits, physical therapy sessions and court proceedings to last several lifetimes. But they loved their son, and that's what you do when you love someone. That choice wasn't his to make.

Jason couldn't bare the strain he was inflicting on his parents. He saw it growing on their faces every day, but he was helpless to change it. They tried not to talk in front of him about the bills and the sacrifices they have made, but sometimes he could hear them talking at night. Besides, he wasn't a baby anymore; he fully understood the commitment they have made to him. It's been a long three months and he hasn't seen any rainbows with pots of gold at the other end, or a light shining at the end of any tunnels. All he could see was darkness.

He found little solace in his room. He had his music and his video games; they managed to keep his mind occupied for awhile at least. But no matter what he did he couldn't escape the devastation he caused that night. The night he ran head-on into Will and Joey Bradley, and changed the lives of two families forever. He would have to live with the knowledge of what he did for the rest of his life.

The fact that he might never walk again was only the smallest part of it. He took Sarah Bradley's family away from her, not to mention ruining his parents financially and emotionally. He would gladly give up the use of his legs forever if he could only change what happened that night. But he couldn't, and now he has to find a way to live with himself.

Underneath his mattress he kept a scrapbook of old family photos, school awards... and the newspaper clipping from the accident. He forced himself to look at it every single day. He never wanted to forget what he did... and he never would. This wheelchair was a constant reminder.

He read the headline to himself, hoping that it had somehow magically changed to read something more pleasant. But it was still the same.

~ Teen Kills Father and Son in
Head-On Collision ~

Reporters have a talent for exploiting the obvious, that's for sure. But the accident was nothing more than just that...an accident. Jason wasn't drunk, he wasn't on drugs. Nor was he speeding or listening to a blaring, bass thumping radio. He was alone and on his way home from work when he dropped his cell phone. He bent down to pick it up and jerked the wheel into the opposite lane.

Day and night he saw the accident over and over again in his head, playing out in slow motion like a movie.

He grabs the phone and straightens up just in time to see Will's car crash through his front end. The cold, hard metal from both vehicles buckling at the moment of impact and melding together like soft clay, defying physics at its fundamental core.

That stupid phone! Two people dead and so many lives changed forever because he dropped his phone! Everyday choices are made, and not always the right ones. The hardest part is living with the consequences of those choices... forever.

There was a soft knock on his door. It had to be his mom, dad rarely knocked.

"Come in," he answered.

"Hi honey, how are you feeling today? Are you hungry? I have dinner on, it's your favorite. Lasagna," She's rambling, something's up.

"Cool, yeah I can definitely eat. Thanks mom," he replied.

"Hey, um... there's something I need to tell you, but I don't want you to get upset," the look on her face was filled with bad news.

"If you start out like that then I know it's not good. What is it?" he didn't want to know, he was sure of it.

"Um... Sarah Bradley... died last week. It was in the paper today, her neighbor found her," she choked the words out of her lumped-up throat.

"Oh mom... NO! How? What happened?" tears were welling in his eyes. He was trying to stay composed, but his voice was betraying him.

"Um... she OD'd on some pills," her voice was cracking as she spoke.

"On purpose?" he couldn't contain his composure any longer, he was crying now.

"No one knows; she didn't leave any kind of a note. Her doctor had her on all kinds of medication, it could have been an accident," her attempt to reassure her son wasn't working. She wasn't even sure she believed that herself.

"It was no accident. I killed her! It was my fault! I killed that whole entire family! Me!" his sobbing was completely out of control. He was totally devastated by this news, just when he thought things couldn't get any worse. But somehow they always do.

There was no doubt in his mind that the events of that fatal night led to Sarah's death. He couldn't deny it if he wanted to. He refused to deny it. How could he ever live with himself now?

"Oh baby... I'm so sorry. I wish I could change everything, but I can't," she was holding her son so tight, doing everything in a mother's power to console her hurting child.

"Me too mommy," he said, hanging on to his mom for dear life. They sat there for what could have been an eternity, just holding each other, and cried.

Why does life have to be so hard? Everything is supposed to be fun and easy when you're a kid. But it doesn't always work out the way it should, sometimes life has a funny way of playing out. The true test of faith is how you handle the things that life throws your way. This was a lesson that seventeen year old Jason Stevens had to learn the hard way... and it could break him.

CHAPTER 13

Salvation City was in its typical state of busy chatter. There were angels as far as the eye could see, flashing in, flashing out and floating from floor to floor. Most would just congregate together and laugh and talk about all sorts of things. Their assignments, life, death, people they left behind, missing their past lives and waiting for their redemption.

Although they were no longer *living* in the literal earthly sense, they were still very much alive. They still possessed all their feelings of love and compassion for each other, guiding them just as it did during their life in the mortal world, but with one great advantage. All the destructive emotions that had control over them on earth were no longer a part of their lives here. They were completely liberated.

With the exception of Leo and David making regular appearances to drop off new souls or dole out assignments, their days were pretty uneventful; but every once in awhile they got the rare opportunity to glimpse the changing of the guard for the *Angels of War.* They were so glorious and awesome that the chance to witness them marching through *Salvation City* was quite a breathtaking experience.

This was one of those days.

At the east end of the main hall the golden doors began to silently open. As they unfurled a brilliant, pure white light spilled through the crack like a burst of sunlight breaking through the clouds. The doors slowly opened wider and the white light filled the entire entrance; blinding anyone from seeing inside the luminous void.

All conversation in *Salvation City* ceased. Angels stopped all flight and began to gather around the main hall. Sarah joined the others to see what was going on, but all she could see was an incredibly bright light.

Sarah looked up at the other floors and saw that every bit of space around the encompassing balconies was occupied with silent angels leaning over the side in anticipation. They watched with quiet reverence as they waited patiently for a glimpse of the glorious site to come.

"What's going on?" she whispered to Nigel.

"The *Angels of War* are changing out their guard," he replied.

"What are the *Angels of War?*" she asked.

"You'll see," answered Maggie.

"They're so beautiful," said Calista.

Shadows could now be seen moving in the light and gradually became distinguishable figures. They started to immerge through the white light in the doorway and stood side by side in a row fifty wide. Their soft footsteps could be heard marching in unison, growing louder as they drew closer to the entrance of the main hall. As they crossed the threshold of the golden double doors they came into full view, the light no longer hiding them from their audience. They were in perfect formation, each one poised the same as the next, moving together as one.

Resembling ancient Spartan soldiers, the *Angels of War* were suited from head to toe in pure gold body armor. Each angel had and identical golden shield carved with an intricate cross inlaid with pure silver. They were armed with a golden sword that was sheathed on their left side and in their right hand they carried a long golden spear.

But it was their wings that were the most spectacular thing Sarah had ever seen. Although Vinchetto's wings were beautiful, they couldn't compare to those of the *Angels of War*. They weren't hidden like the *angels of redemptions'* wings; they were in plain view and were the purest white she'd ever seen. Their wings reached high above their heads by at least a couple of feet and stopped just short of the floor behind them.

These were the angels she had always pictured in Sunday school, but could only hope were real. And now she knew. She had the honor to actually see their beauty and glory with her own eyes. She reached up to her face, totally overwhelmed with emotion, and realized that she was crying.

They continued to file through the main hall, row after row of these glorious soldiers. They had to be at least a hundred rows deep before anyone saw their end and the golden doors slowly began to draw closed. They vanished with a brilliant flash of light, row by row, just before reaching the other set of golden doors at the west end of the main hall.

After the last of the *Angels of War* disappeared, heading to their final destination, silence draped over everyone in *Salvation City* like a heavy blanket. There were no words or emotions that could describe the reverence they commanded by just their mere presence. The respect they received from their fellow angels was earned many times over by the sacrifices they had made over the centuries. They were, in every sense of the word, the truly righteous.

Nigel looked over at Sarah and saw the tears running down her face. He smiled and said, "They have quite an effect, don't they?"

She was completely speechless. She just looked at him and nodded.

"Everyone has the same reaction the first time they get the honor of seeing the *Angels of War* come through *Salvation City*," he said.

The whole group looked at her and smiled. They remembered the first time they saw this amazing sight.

"Come on Sarah," said Calista and they both headed back to their sitting room.

"Hey Calista, can I ask you something?" said Sarah, wiping the leftover tears from her face.

"Uh… sure," Calista wasn't quite sure what to expect. She didn't want to be cornered with a question she wasn't ready to answer just yet.

"Can we travel wherever we want? I mean... you know, if we want to see someone we left behind?"

"Well of course, you can go wherever you want. But I don't suggest it," she answered, relieved that Sarah didn't ask who was with her when she died.

"Why not?" Sarah asked.

"'Cause you can never go *back*. If you spend too much time dwelling on the people or the life you left behind it can be very dangerous."

"Did you go *back*?"

"Well yeah, we all have. Some stay longer than they should, but most of us manage to find our way back here. One way or another."

Sarah thought about this for a moment and just stared into the fireplace thinking of past things. Her life, her death, her first assignment, seeing her family again. It all seemed so surreal, like some kind of dream that you can't wake up from. The dream isn't a bad dream, but it's a dream just the same.

She didn't leave much behind, but she needed some kind of closure. Sarah thought that maybe seeing what she left behind would remind her of what lies ahead. She was so confused; all this was so much to accept.

The truth is she didn't know what to do or think. Sarah believed that she would be with Will and Joey right now, but instead she found herself in a decaying, empty house with this new life as her only option to see her family again. Sarah knew it would probably be a mistake to try to go back and see what she left behind, but she felt she no choice at this point. She had to go back.

CHAPTER 14

"She's gone!" yelled Calista as she ran toward Nigel and the others.

"What? Who's gone?" he asked. "Slow down and talk to me."

"Sarah, she's gone," said Calista in a panic. "I can't find her anywhere."

"I'm sure she's around here somewhere," replied Vinchetto.

"The other day, after the *Angels of War* came through, she asked me all kinds of questions about being able to go *back*."

"And what did you say?" asked Maggie.

"I told her we can go wherever we want, of course. I had to tell her the truth!" Calista exclaimed.

"Alright, no one start to worry just yet. She hasn't been gone long and it's not like all of us haven't gone *back* ourselves," Nigel reassured them. "If she's gone too long we'll go out to find her. It won't be too difficult; there aren't very many places she would go."

Vinchetto and Calista looked at each other with worry on their minds. They both felt responsible for Sarah and couldn't let her slide down that slippery slope. Not when she's already come this far. They would give her some time, a few days in *mortal* time, and then they would find her and bring her back home.

For some angels, this was what was needed in order for them to let go of their *mortal life* on earth and be at peace with their *eternal life*. Sometimes the hardest part of death isn't the life that's left behind, but the life that lies ahead. It's a real leap of faith for those who are afraid to let go. That could be why so many souls linger in the mortal world and won't cross over. Fear of the unknown can be crippling... even for the dead.

ζ

Sarah wasn't sure why she wanted to go back to her old house so badly, but for some reason she was drawn to it like the pull of the earth's gravity. She arrived in exactly the same spot where she and David had left, in the middle of her lonely, deserted bedroom.

It was dusk now and the pinkish, orange glow from the setting sun outside stained the room red. She could see faint dust particles floating in the room where the remaining daylight crept through the bedroom window.

Someone had already been here and started to pack up all their things. The bedding and pillows were gone and only the bare mattress laid witness to the happy couple that once lived here. The pictures had all been removed from the dresser and nightstands and were peaking out of the opened packing boxes that were scattered all over the room. The walls were bare and the drapes were gone, this room no longer resembled a home.

She walked into the bathroom and sat on the side of the tub where she died. She ran her hand along the smooth, cool porcelain and the feelings that drove her to that final act of desperation now flooded her mind. Coming here brought back all the memories and raw emotions that she so desperately tried to escape. Sarah was starting to think maybe this wasn't such a good idea after all, but she had to finish this. If she wanted to be able to let go and move on, if she ever wanted to see her Will and Joey again, she would have to be able to give up this world.

Sarah went into Joey's room. Aside from the mural of outer space on the wall, the room no longer looked like the bedroom of a child... her child. The same scene of half packed boxes, bare windows and an empty mattress haunted this once happy room.

Sarah looked around and saw sticking out of one of the boxes an old, brown teddy bear. Joey had slept with this bear every night from the time he was only three. It was a little bald in some spots and was missing an eye, but it was loved just the same. She leaned down and touched the bear, it was still so soft.

She had to leave this place; it was no longer the home she remembered. The missing pictures, the packed up toys and discarded belonging... the absent family. This house was nothing more than just that... a *house*. It was no longer the home of the Bradley family.

Sarah went to the living room and took one last look around. This room was the same as the others, deserted and empty. Swallowing the painful memories that she so desperately wanted to forget she closed her eyes tightly. With a cool rush of wind and a flash of light she left this place... forever.

ζ

Sarah didn't go back to *Salvation City*. Not yet anyway. Her destination was the final resting place for her and her lost family. Four headstones, side by side. Poppy, Will, Joey and now Sarah all lay together forever, one family gone from this world and on to the next. Well, that was the plan anyway. Sarah's final destination would be determined by her... and her alone.

She had to make things right again, the people she loved so much in life were waiting for her. She needed them more than anything now, all the love she had for them in life she carried with her in death. Her heart forever sealed to theirs.

Sarah sat down on the thick, green grass and stared at Will's and Joey's headstones. The flowers on their graves were completely dead now. The flowers at her headstone were wilting, but still intact, just barely hanging on. Not for much longer though. The flowers were a perfect reflection of her last days. Barely alive, letting nature take its course while they waited to join with the other flowers that had already died. Paralleled circumstances.

As Sarah sat there contemplating her past and her future, time continued. The sun set and rose around her several times, as if someone had sped up the frames of movie. The time to her only seemed like minutes, but that was the beauty of being eternal. You literally have all the time in the world.

She watched people come and go, bringing flowers to lost loved ones. Some would stay awhile, others only briefly. But two people in particular soon caught her attention. They were heading in her direction so she watched to see where they would go. It was a woman with a young man in wheelchair.

Sarah stood up.

She knew immediately who they were. Jason Stevens and his mother Joanne. Joanne was pushing her son across the grass as he bumped along on the uneven terrain. In his arms he was holding flowers... lots of them. Sarah put her hand to her mouth; it hadn't even occurred to her what her death would do to this poor young boy.

She had tried so hard to hate him, but he was so torn apart over what he had done that he hated himself enough for the both of them. She just watched as they drew closer to the row of headstones that entombed an entire family.

He was so pale and his eyes were swollen and red. Tears had stained his cheeks as he tried to keep himself composed. The closer he got the harder it was for him to hold it together.

Jason Stevens, this broken young man, carried the weight of the world on his shoulders and Sarah's death was the final straw. He began to cry, unable to control himself. His mother gently put her hands on his shoulders to assure him that he wasn't alone.

"Sarah," his voice was cracking as he spoke. "I'm so sorry! Can you ever forgive me?"

Sarah was completely overwhelmed with emotions of guilt and sorrow for this poor tortured soul. She kneeled before him as she reached out and touched him, but he couldn't feel her hand on his face. The depth of his pain was so intense that Sarah could feel it penetrate to her very core. He was in a bad way and Sarah didn't know what to do. She just wanted to take his pain away and tell him it would be alright, but she didn't know how.

"Jason," Sarah whispered into his ear. "I forgive you." Jason started to cry harder, his sobbing was quickly out of control.

"I'm so, so sorry," he whispered over and over again.

"You have to forgive yourself now," Sarah said to him as she continued to caress his face. Jason's mom put the flowers in front of the three headstones. His crying had subsided a bit, but it still had a pretty good hold over him.

"Mom?" Jason turned to look at Joanne. "Do you think they're ok?"

"Yes baby, I do," she was crying too. "They're all together now. That's all she wanted. To be with them... with her family."

"Soon Jason," said Sarah. "I'll be with them soon, don't you worry." Sarah leaned over and kissed Jason's forehead.

They stayed for a little while longer and mourned for the family that was now gone forever. Jason grabbed his mom's hand and squeezed it.

"Ok mom, I'm ready."

"Are you sure?" his mom asked.

"Yes," he replied with hesitance. Joanne turned her son's wheelchair around and started him back across the bumpy path they came in on.

Jason turned back to look at the headstones. Sarah watched him. "Goodbye Sarah... Please forgive me," he said.

Sarah watched them until they were completely out of sight. She was ready to go back now; this was what she needed to move on. She took one last look at the family that rested here and said, "See you soon." She blew them a kiss and went home to *Salvation City*.

CHAPTER 15

The view from the top floor office was nothing less than breathtaking. The Las Vegas strip at dusk from forty floors up bears witness to the true essence of Vegas in all its colorful, lit-up glory. Sin City at its finest.

Steven Carvell leaned back in his leather office chair and stared out at the beautiful city that hustled and bustled below him. His executive office suited his executive lifestyle with all its leather chairs, mahogany lined walls and bookshelves, and the huge desk made of glass and steel. Behind his desk was a floor to ceiling window that stretched the entire width of his office and overlooked the famous Las Vegas strip.

He had worked long and hard over the years, selling himself... and his soul... to get to this station in life. But now it was all slipping away faster than he could stop it. His life was on a runaway train and completely out of his control.

In his hands was the letter of termination he received from the board members today. He had read it and re-read it at least a hundred times. How could they do this to him? He had given his blood, sweat and tears to this blasted company for the past decade... and for what? The first sign of trouble and they give him his walking papers.

He was under investigation for embezzlement, along with several others, and the company wanted to sever all ties with those involved. Whether they were all guilty or not. How could this even happen? He was Steven Carvell; he was above these petty charges!

Steven stewed over his situation; anger and frustration were burning a hole in his stomach and filling him with hate. Steven, however, was completely oblivious to the uninvited guests that now lingered in his office. Hell's *soldiers* occupied this office now.

The bookshelves were covered with the dead, decaying *crows* of Satan. They would flutter their wings and caw randomly, as if in conversation with each other. *Soldier* demons perched themselves on the backs of his chairs, digging their talons into the fine, supple leather. They would slink around on the floor, taking flight occasional and swooping towards Steven, making him uneasy.

Steven's assistant knocked on his office door. "Come in," hollered Steven.

"Mr. Carvell, I'm sorry to disturb you sir, but I need your signature on these invoices please." Holly Jacobs had the most uncomfortable feeling in this office tonight. She quickly placed the papers in front of Steven so she wouldn't have to stay too long. She didn't always feel this way; normally he was fairly pleasant to be around. But there was something not quite right going on. She couldn't put her finger on it, but it was there none the less.

Steven signed the last of the invoices and asked, "Is there anything else tonight Holly?"

"No sir. I'll have those documents you requested ready for you in the morning," she looked around the office as if trying to catch a glimpse of a ghost. The hairs on the back of her neck stood up and she could swear that someone was standing right behind her.

"Great Holly, thank you. Why don't you go home. It's been a long day and you've been working really hard lately," said Steven. He was really fond Holly; she was efficient and always pleasant to be around. Not bad on the eyes either, if anyone ever asked.

"Thank you Mr. Carvell. Do you want me to bring you anything before I leave?" she asked as she quickly scooped up the papers he had just signed.

"Nope, I'm good. Have a good night," he said. "Oh, and Holly."

"Yes sir?"

"Tell Rick I said 'hello'." Rick was her husband and a really great guy. He didn't always have the best of luck with jobs, but he tried really hard and he adored his wife. Steven admired him for that. Even though Steven had all this *so-called* success, he had to sacrifice his family to get it. Rick always put Holly first. Although they didn't have much money they were always happy. Besides, they always seemed to have what they needed, and that was the way it was supposed to be. Wasn't it?

She smiled at him and replied, "I will. Good night sir," she turned and headed out the door. That was the last time he ever intended to see sweet Holly again.

Steven walked over to his bar and poured himself a pretty healthy shot of scotch. No ice and no water, just straight up. He inhaled it down in one swift gulp and then he made himself another. The demons love it when the *mortals* drink; it makes their job so much easier.

Satan's minions grew restless. The *soldiers* took flight and looped all around Steven. The *crows* started in with their chilling caws and flapped their wings with unrest. More of the vile creatures started to make their appearance in the room in anticipation of the inevitable fate that laid ahead for Steven Carvell.

Still completely unaware of the unwelcome guests that surrounded him, Steven experienced an indescribable feeling of anxiety. If only he could see the unpleasant creatures that impatiently awaited the harvest of his soul he might have made different choices in his life. For Steven, the ultimate battle to save not only his mortal being, but his eternal soul would soon be underway.

But the demons wouldn't give him up that easily, they had been waiting to take him to Hell for some time now and their chance was finally here. Fortunately for Steven he would have quite a team of redeemers that wouldn't give him up without a fight. Steven Carvell's life was about to change one way or the other... forever.

CHAPTER 16

"Welcome back Sarah," said Nigel smiling. He was leaning on one of the stone columns watching as Sarah appeared into the main hall from her recent adventure into the past. She looked at him and smiled.

"What did you find?" he asked her.

She thought about it for a moment and replied, "Freedom."

"Good answer, that's what I was hoping you would find. Not everyone does," he walked toward her and continued. "Many souls find themselves lost to their past when they try to go *back*."

"I have to admit, I worried about that myself," she replied.

"What freed you?"

"I went to the family gravesite and I realized that the only one lost was me. I couldn't do that to my family," she paused and said, "Hell, I couldn't do that to myself! I killed myself because I wanted to be with them again.

I didn't leave them there, I left them *here.* So you see, I had to come back."

"Good for you Sarah," said Nigel. "I just want you to know that I never doubted you, not for one second."

"Oh really?" she asked.

"Not me, but Vinchetto sure did. Yeah, he swore he was going to have to track you down and drag you back," Nigel chuckled.

"Yeah sure, whatever," countered Sarah.

"What, you don't believe me? Ask him yourself then."

"I will," she laughed.

"Go ahead," Nigel smiled. "Just so you know, I'm not afraid of Vinchetto. Oh sure, he's scary and all, but I'm pretty sure I can take him."

"Maybe, but I might have to take that bet," she said. Nigel put his hand on her shoulder and they went into their gathering room where the others anxiously jumped up to greet Sarah.

Maggie and Calista were the first to reach her. Calista threw her arms around Sarah and hugged her. Maggie just hung back a bit and let Calista pour out her relief over Sarah's return.

"I'm so glad you're back," expressed Calista, smiling from ear to ear.

"We're all glad you're back. We've gotten quite attached to you," smiled Maggie. For some strange reason every time Sarah looked at Maggie she pictured a lit cigarette hanging out of her mouth and a cup of coffee in her hand. Those must have been her vices back in the mortal world.

"I knew you'd be back kid," said Vinchetto.

"Really? That's not what Nigel said," Sarah smiled and looked over at Nigel. He urged her to be quiet and then looked around causally and started to whistle when Vinchetto turned toward him.

"Is that so?" said Vinchetto, more of a statement than a question. He looked over at Nigel who was still acting casual and punched him on the arm.

Nigel grabbed at his arm where Vinchetto hit him and rubbed it in vain. He said, "It's a good thing we don't feel pain around here." They both looked at each other and laughed.

"Hey everyone, Leo's going to have an assignment ready soon. This one will be for Maggie and Sarah. Vinchetto will be going with you though," said Nigel, back to business in the blink of an eye.

"What kind of assignment?" asked Maggie.

"A *jumper* in Las Vegas," Nigel replied.

"Oh man, I hate the *jumpers!*" said Maggie as she started to become very uneasy.

"None of us like the *jumpers*, but I was told this one is specifically for you Maggie. Vinchetto will be with you and if you need any back up just *call.*"

If the *angels of redemption* were ever in trouble or needed re-enforcements they could call on their fellow angels to come to their aid. In order for them to call on other angels they had to recite a phrase. The phrase went straight to the hearts of all the *angels of redemption*, no matter where they were or what they were doing.

It was simple enough.

Fellow angels
Souls in arms
I need you now
To save from harm

"Yeah, I know. Alright, when is Leo going to give us the rundown?" Maggie asked.

"Soon, I'm actually surprised he hasn't already called on us." No sooner had Nigel spoken these words when Leo appeared in all his grandeur.

"Hello my angels," came the overpowering voice of their gracious *Proctor.*

ζ

It didn't take long for this well oiled machine of warriors to get geared up and transported to their assignment. This was only Sarah's second assignment, but she had been witness to a pretty intense scene last time. This time it was only one guy.

How bad could it be?

When they arrived the room was already filled with *crows* and *soldiers.* The nasty creatures were up to their typical screeching and clawing tactics. They were a menace in every sense of the word. The air in the room was thick with the stench of sulfur and a dark haze had already begun to absorb the light. The Prince of Darkness had his slaves well trained in the art of gloom and doom, and they were quite the efficient task masters.

Sitting in one of the leather chairs facing Steven's desk was a *higher level* demon. He had his fingers interlocked across his chest and his feet up on the desk staring out the window at the glorious view of Sin City. He felt quite at home here, in this town full of corruption and despair.

Standing next to Steven was another *higher level* demon that Sarah had never seen before. The one in the chair was Arzulu, the same demon that fought Vinchetto at the Grayson house. But the one next to their *mortal* was a woman, if they even had men and women demons in the biblical sense.

She was extremely tall and slender and her appearance wasn't quite as terrifying as Barthalius and Arzulu. Her features, although still quite hideous, were much more refined. Her teeth weren't razors, they were human with the exception that they were stained a horribly sick brownish, yellow. Her lips were deep red instead of black and she had long, silver hair. Her cheeks were sunken in and her eyes were the same solid black, lifeless marbles as the others, but you could tell that this demon was definitely more feminine than the other *higher levels* Sarah had seen.

Vinchetto's guard was up immediately. He could fight two *higher levels* if he had to, but he wouldn't be able to keep the minions' of Hell's influence away from their *mortal* while he did.

Maggie and Sarah were both here, but this other *higher level* preferred a sword like Arzulu. Maggie's weapons of choice were handguns, and no match for the demon's skill with a blade. Sarah would be forced to fight one of the *higher levels* while Maggie battled the *soldiers* and the *crows*.

No, this wasn't going to work. They would have to *call* for re-enforcements if they were going to win this one.

"What's the matter Vinchetto? Are you feeling a little outnumbered?" Arzulu didn't even turn around to look at him when he spoke.

"I think you you're the ones that are outnumbered," replied Vinchetto. "I only count two of you and there are one, two, three of us," he said as he looked at the others and took a head count.

"Are you forgetting my *soldiers*?"

Without blinking an eye Vinchetto drew his sword and spun it around over his head and in a figure eight pattern, taking out three

110

soldiers that were flapping around his head while he stood there. They disappeared with a deafening screech into a puff of black smoke and dust.

"What *soldiers?*" Vinchetto asked with his mobster charm.

"You think you're so clever don't you... Vinchetto?" Arzulu finally turned to look at him. "I seem to remember how clever you thought you were when you were alive too. So cocky and arrogant. Don't get me wrong... I like that in a man," he smiled and revealed his jagged, razor teeth.

"Well, you know, I don't like to blow my horn or anything, but I was pretty clever back in the day," his casual attitude only elevated Arzulu's aggravation. This was exactly what Vinchetto wanted. He looked over at the girls and said, "Stay sharp ladies. And Sarah, watch out for Nadira, she's all yours."

Swords were drawn and Arzulu leaped out of the chair toward Vinchetto. Maggie pulled out both of her guns and unleashed a relentless barrage of bullets on the disgusting, rotting *crows*. Nadira drew her sword as she came at Sarah with lightening speed. Sarah pulled her swords from their sheaths and took this *higher level* demon head-on.

111

The sharp clash of steel on steel filled the room. Its heavy atmosphere of sulfur and grey dust from the defeated *soldiers* and *crows* grew thicker by the minute.

All the while Steven Carvell was totally unaware of the war that was raging over the ownership rights of his corrupted soul. Right here in the very same room where he now stood and contemplated his own mortality.

CHAPTER 17

The *call* came in and every soul in *Salvation City* stood motionless. Within a single instant they moved as one machine and readied themselves to join their fellow angels' in arms. Nigel and Calista headed for the weapons room and suited up, they were quickly joined by Natalia's and Brad's teams.

Angels didn't send out the *call* very often… especially Vinchetto. This had to be big. Other's floated down from the upper floors and geared up as well, everyone knew that if Vinchetto *called* for help then all Hell had to be breaking loose… literally.

The first wave of re-enforcements was on their way. Only two full teams, plus Nigel and Calista would come to their side for now, but hundreds more were ready to join in when needed. An *angel* cavalry.

Calista's and Nigel's main concern was for Sarah. She was still so new and even though she was adjusting well they worried that she didn't have the skills she needed to defend herself against Satan's ruthless minions. If Sarah was up against a *higher level* she might not be able to hold it off, let alone defeat it.

Sarah's skill with her swords was remarkable, but some of the *higher level* demons were centuries old, even thousands of years old, and she was no match for their experience. Her single mission and training time with Vinchetto couldn't even come close to the field time of Satan's first string players. Yes... they were worried alright.

Natalia's team, Brad's team, Nigel and Calista moved quickly to join forces with their fellow redeemers. They had no idea what fury had been unleashed in the heart of Sin City, but they were preparing for the worst. If more of God's warriors were needed then they would be ready to depart in a moment's notice, but for now Nigel hoped that they would be enough to end whatever conflict was escalating out of Vinchetto's control.

ζ

The top floor office with the spectacular view now resembled the *Seventh Circle of Hell*. The heavy haze from the black smoke of the fallen minions filtered out most of the light and was so thick it could have been cut with a knife. The gagging stench of hot sulfur would have been enough to knock any *mortal* unconscious. It was a good thing they couldn't actually inhale the suffocating substance.

Nigel looked around the room and took a quick inventory of the situation. There were six *higher levels*, more than a dozen *soldiers,* and what could easily have been two hundred of Hell's rotting *crows*.

But what really caught Nigel's attention were the four *reapers* that were twisting and curling their long, cat-like bodies around the *mortal,* who was staring blankly out the window at the moving world below. Oblivious to the chaos that now surrounded every inch of him, Steven stood motionless, as if glued to the very spot he was standing, boiling over with anger and consumed with self-pity.

Reapers have one purpose and one purpose *only...* soul collection. This *mortal* wasn't just in danger of losing his life; he was losing his soul too. Steven Carvell was damned in every sense of the word.

The *reapers* had bodies like long, stretched black cats with no tails. They slinked around their prey and wrapped their twisting bodies around the legs and torsos of their unsuspecting quarry. Their heads, however, looked more like that of a bat. They had glowing red eyes and a lipless mouth that exposed their jagged, deadly fangs with unrelenting terror. Their ears lay flat against their heads and black saliva dripped from their ghoulish teeth. They were, without question, one of Satan's most despicable offspring.

When their victims are ready to be harvested the *reapers* use their sharp, thick claws and their fierce fangs to tear the screaming, tortured souls from their bodies. Not a single inch is left untouched. The shredded, ravaged souls experience nothing but shear pain and agony in their last moments before being dragged to their eternal damnation into the bowels of Hell.

The sight was nearly unbearable for the redeemers to witness. When the *reapers* were present at an assignment the *angels of redemption* were desperate to change the fate of the *mortal*. No one deserved a fate as hideous as that... well, almost no one.

116

Vinchetto and his nemesis, Arzulu, were going at it tooth and nail, along with another *higher level* named Borm. He was a nasty customer, but *Vinnie the Bull* seemed to have a handle on the two *higher levels*... for now.

Maggie was backed into a corner blasting away at anything and everything. She was holding off a *higher level* along with half a dozen *soldiers* that swooped and lunged at her. She was one tough old bird and Nigel found it hard to believe that she would have given up so easily in the mortal world. But he was glad to have her on his team just the same.

Sarah was the one he was really worried about, but when he found her in the dim haze of the overcrowded room he saw that she was holding her own against a *higher level*. And not just any *higher level*, but Nadira none the less. Nadira had taken out her fair share of redeemers, but she seemed to have met her match in this shy, uncertain warrior newly recruited to the cause of *soul salvation*.

The two remaining *higher levels* watched with sheer pleasure as their fellow demons seemed to be engaged in what could be considered at first sight as certain victory. As the redeemers began to appear one by one to unite with their brothers' and sisters' in arms the atmosphere in the room began to shift. The *soldiers* and *crows* took notice immediately, and cawed and screeched in panic. They took flight from their perches, teeth and talons exposed, and targeted the new arrivals in an attempt to intimidate. But they were grossly outmatched.

The two *higher levels* that were previously observing their *certain victory* in amusement were no longer bound to their positions of overwhelming confidence. They jumped up to meet their opposition and were greeted by no less than twelve *angels of redemption.*

"Hi there," said Natalia with a grin so big her white teeth could light up a small village. Natalia loved to battle. She was in her element here and it showed.

"Let's rock and roll!" shouted Joshua as he drew his two Japanese tachi swords and twisted his wrists around as if he were twirling batons. His swords spun around at his sides in big looping circles. The *higher level* demon named Sumann drew his sword and came at Joshua without hesitation.

The deafening crash of the steel when the swords connected sliced through the room. Natalia and Nigel had their swords drawn and quickly joined in the battle. Nigel took on Borm to relieve Vinchetto from his two on one fight, and Natalia was met head on by Barthalius. Samuel came to Maggie's aid and diverted the attention of the *higher level*, Razula, that had Maggie pinned in the corner.

The room took on the ancient tradition of the Roman gladiators and their battles to the death. Good versus evil, angels' versus demons... this fight was inherently elemental, never changing since the beginning of time.

CHAPTER 18

Steven Carvell made himself another stiff drink. That was the last thing he needed, but the numbing affect from the alcohol seemed to be curbing his anxiety for the moment. He walked around his desk and sat down for what could be the last time ever and looked at the pictures that resided there.

Captured forever in their youthful beauty were his two babies. Levi was fifteen now, and little Cadence was only five. Oh how he loved these two kids. He couldn't understand how such tiny, little babies could have such a huge impact on the heart of a grown man. Yet somehow they did. And as the babies grow, so does their hold over you. Amazing!

How could everything have gone so wrong?

Over the years his only intention, his sole mission in life, was to provide a better life for his wife, Katie, and their two kids. But he got so caught up in the lifestyle and the big money that he forgot what really mattered. Now that lifestyle was gone. The family, the money, the job... gone... all of it. All the dirty dealings and his indiscretions had come back to bite him, and it was time to pay the piper.

Steven knew he has made some bad choices over the years, and hurt a lot of innocent people in the process, but he did it all for his family. Doesn't that matter? Didn't it make a difference if he did those things for someone other than himself? Of course not! The end doesn't always justify the means.

He picked up the picture of his kids. He held it in his hands and whispered, "It was all for you. I'm so sorry I failed you." He put the picture back on the desk and opened his desk drawer. He took his keys out of the drawer and closed it back up. He fumbled the keys around in his hand and contemplated his next move... his final move.

Steven rose from his chair and headed for the door. He slowly made his way down the hall to the stairwell. He could have taken the elevator to the roof, but he needed the extra time. Needed it for what? Did he want to talk himself out of something? Clear his head maybe? He didn't know what he would do once he reached the roof, but he knew quite clearly what his intentions were.

Steven climbed the stairs, each step slow and deliberate. He couldn't stop thinking about that letter; it was forever etched in his mind. Over and over he had read the letter. The letter that would ruin him and his family financially. It still hadn't even occurred to him that he might go to jail over this. None of that mattered now anyway.

Another step, slower than the last. It was as if he was waiting for someone, or *something*, to swoop in and stop him. But he was all alone in the stairwell, suffocating on his own desperation. His feet felt like they were treading through molasses, each step harder than the one before. He didn't know what he was doing anymore, but he believed he had no other options at this point. His choices were taken off the table and now he had to take the only way out he knew.

Another step... almost there now.

ζ

Petite, little Cadence sat on the floor in her bedroom playing with her baby doll. It only took her a moment to notice the visitor that had sat down beside her. She looked up at her visitor and smiled.

"Hi," said Cadence.

"Hello there," responded Sophie.

"What's your name?"

"My name is Sophie."

"Are you an *angel* Sophie?" Cadence asked her with the biggest and brightest blue eyes Sophie had ever seen.

"Yes I am," Sophie answered. She continued, "I'm here because I need your help. Someone you love very much is in trouble and he needs the people that love him to help him. Can you do that Cadence? Can you help him?"

"Is it my daddy? He's in trouble, huh?" she asked as if she was not in the least bit surprised by this breaking news.

"Yes Cadence, he is."

"Ok, what do you want me to do?" she asked with all the determination of a grown up, but without any of the doubt or fear.

"You need to call your daddy and tell him you love him. Then ask him when he's coming home," explained Sophie.

"Ok, I'll get my mommy's phone." She stood up and grabbed Sophie by the hand. She pulled Sophie out of her bedroom and into the kitchen with her.

Her mother was standing by the stove making dinner for her and the kids. Cadence walked over to her mother's purse and started to dig through it casually until she found the cell phone. Katie saw her enter the room through the corner of her eye, but paid no attention until she heard Cadence rummaging through her purse. Katie turned to see what this precocious little five year old was up to.

"What do you think you're doing young lady?" Katie asked her daughter.

Cadence continued to take what she needed and paid no attention to her mother's tone. Her tenacity to complete her mission was nothing less than amazing.

"I need to call daddy," she explained in a casual yet serious manner.

"Really, and why do you need to call him little missy?"

"Because the angel told me to," she answered with impatience.

"An angel? What...?" concern was spreading on Katie's face.

"Yes, Sophie the angel. She's right here, don't you see her?" Cadence asked.

"No... do you see her?" her mother moved closer to her, worried that she may be ill or hallucinating.

"Of course I see her, she's standing right here." Cadence pointed to the unoccupied space next to her as her mother put her hand on Cadence's forehead in an attempt to find a fever.

"I'm not sick mommy, I feel fine. I just need to call daddy, he's in trouble and he needs us," she explained to her mother.

"Hey mom?" Levi walked into the kitchen just then.

"Yes honey?" Katie was glad for the brief distraction from the disturbing conversation with her daughter.

"I think we need to call dad, I get a weird feeling that something has happened," Levi's face was shrouded with confusion and concern.

"Levi has an angel too," Cadence said to her mother. "What's your name?" she asked the empty space next to Levi.

"Cadence, what are you doing?" Her mother was starting to panic and all the color drained from her face. She didn't know what to do with her delusional daughter. But Cadence paid no attention to her mother; she was deep in conversation with the two angels that were sent to Steven Carvell's family to intervene in his last desperate act.

"Ok, it's time to call your father," Katie hit the speed dial on her cell phone and called her ex-husband. She had no idea what was going on here, but something in her heart told her that, whether she believed it or not, there was an act of divine intervention going on here that couldn't be ignored.

"Steven?" she said. "The kids wanted to call you. Is everything alright?"

Sophie and Brad looked at each other with relief. Brad reached down to little Cadence and brushed her cheek with the back of his hand.

"Good job sweetheart," he said to Cadence. Sophie and Brad smiled at her and she smiled proudly back at her visiting angels.

CHAPTER 19

Steven stood at the edge of the roof and peered over the side at the seemingly endless abyss directly below. The only thing separating him from a descent to certain death was an eighteen inch parapet wall. His cell phone rang and he was grateful for the distraction... saved by the bell.

He looked at the caller-id and saw that it was Katie. Had she known what was happening to him? Could she feel his despair? Despite the turn that their marriage has now taken, it could never change the history between them. Their bond, although now broken, would always give them the intuition and connection they once shared.

"Katie, why are you calling me? Are the kids alright?" he asked.

"The kids are fine. The question is, are you?"

He paused a moment. "I got fired today," he confessed.

"Because of the charges?" she asked, but that question didn't really require an answer. She already knew what would happen when she heard about the embezzlement charge. She wasn't surprised that charges like these had been filed in the first place. Katie always knew that Steven's actions would catch up with him sooner or later. She just hoped that *sooner or later* would never come.

"Yeah," he replied.

"Well, the kids wanted to talk to you. Cadence said an *angel* told her to call you, and even Levi said he had a feeling that we should call you too," she took a deep breath and paused for a moment. "So what's really going on?"

"Nothing's going on," he lied. "I'm just thinking that's all. You know... about... things."

"You always were a horrible liar," she answered him with a stern tone. "We're coming to pick you up. You can have dinner at home with us tonight."

"No, don't come down here," he didn't want her and the kids to see the state he was in. Or worse... find his mangled, crushed body on the hotel grounds somewhere.

"Why not?" she asked.

"I don't want to leave my car here," he answered quickly. "I'll come up to the house when I'm done. I still have some things to sort through here."

"You're so stubborn," she sighed. "Alright then. Someone wants to talk to you first though," Katie handed the phone to Cadence.

"Hi daddy!" Cadence greeted him in her sweet, innocent child's voice.

"Hi baby! Hey, I sure do miss you sweet pea," he was choking back the tears that were welling up in his throat.

"I miss you too daddy. When are you coming home?" she asked in her tiny, little voice.

"Soon baby... soon," he hoped that wasn't a lie, but he felt so desperate and lost that he honestly believed that killing himself would save his family more grief in the end. He couldn't have been more wrong.

"Ok daddy, mommy's making dinner so hurry up."

"Ok sweet pea, I will," he answered. Tears stained his cheeks and he was trying desperately not to let his voice crack.

"I love you daddy," she said. The direct impact of her words were more devastating than a five megaton nuclear bomb.

"I love you too baby," his voice cracked this time. Hopefully his baby girl didn't notice. She wouldn't be able to handle her daddy crying.

He hung up the phone and let the tears flow freely. So many mistakes, so much pain... no way out. What was he going to do? He continued to stare down at the abyss below, torn apart inside with guilt and desperation. If he jumped there would be no turning back... no second chances or calling 911 begging to be rescued. No... this would be it. So he had better be sure.

ζ

The war was raging in full force on the roof now. Vinchetto and Arzulu, Sarah and Nadira, Nigel and Borm, Natalia and Barthalius, Joshua and Sumann, and Samuel and Razula. Each of them battling it out like ancient Samurai Warriors. Maggie, Hannah, Calista and two others from Brad's team were taking on the *soldiers* and the *crows*, swords swinging and guns blaring. The muzzle fire from the guns giving only a brief interruption into the dark night air.

The *reapers* continued to wrap and wind themselves around Steven's body, as if this would ensure the possession of their prize. Mason and Chloe from Brad's team were firing their weapons at the slithering creatures, doing whatever they could to keep the vile beasts off the *mortal.* Even grabbing and ripping at them with their bare hands. But when the *reaper's* will is set, only defeat can break it. And they were not about to let go of Steven Carvell.

Joshua's skill with his tachi swords was beyond excellent, but he seemed to be in over his head with Sumann. This *higher level* was powerful and Joshua was so young and over confident. Joshua's unrelenting will to defeat Sumann kept him feeling strong, but with a swift kick to the chest Sumann had knocked Joshua onto his back about ten feet from where he once stood. He quickly jumped back onto his feet, and without a hitch in his unfaltering attitude he twirled his swords in an act of defiance.

"Impressive... most impressive. But you are not the *Devil* yet!" hollered Joshua to his opponent with a smug grin.

"You talk too much!" Sumann's temper was growing shorter with every word Joshua spoke. "Enough of this! I grow tired of your incessant jabber!" Sumann moved toward Joshua again, but Joshua only smiled and raised his swords in anticipation of Sumann's next move. And the fight continued.

Nigel looked over at Joshua and hoped he could hold out for a little longer, but he appeared to be fairing well for now. It was no different for Sarah. She was handling herself better than most veteran angels against one of the toughest *higher level* demons. They pushed each other back and forth across the roof, never ceasing as their swords hummed through the air with lightening speed. They were so fast that their blades could barely been seen. They were just a brilliant blur of silver streaks whipping across that blackness of the night sky.

Sarah was growing confident, not only with her fighting skills, but with her purpose as an *angel of redemption*. She was beginning to understand the higher calling of their positions and the importance of what they were doing for these lost souls. A second chance doesn't always come easy, so it's important to have someone fighting for you when it does.

As she fought on, anger and anticipation grew with every swing of the sword. Nadira raised her sword and swung it with blinding speed across Sarah's left arm. Sarah couldn't feel any pain, but the use of her arm slowed drastically.

"Ok... I see how you want to play!" Sarah grabbed at her arm and then quickly recovered her composure. "Bring it witch!"

Without a word of response, Nadira lifted her sword in an attempt to end this battle once and for all. Sarah raised her swords straight out to her sides and swung both of her arms forward in one swift motion. She pulled her arms together directly out in front of her, slicing through Nadira's neck as they came together.

Nadira stopped mid swing and her arm dropped to her side. It seemed like an eternity had passed as Nadira looked at Sarah, blinked once, and in slow motion her head slipped off her shoulders and hit the roof top. Sarah stood petrified as she watched the cause and effect of her actions. Nadira's body and head both vanished in a brilliant explosion of flames and black smoke. Every angel and demon stood motionless as the event unfolded before their eyes.

Vinchetto watched this in amazement and suddenly burst out laughing.

"Not so tough now, are you?" Vinchetto could barely contain his laughter.

"So you thinks that's amusing, do you?" asked Arzulu.

"Are you kidding? I think it's funny as hell!" he replied, not missing a beat in his fight against Arzulu.

"Really... how about this?" Arzulu sprinted toward Steven, who was standing directly next to the parapet wall at the edge of the roof. With a brutal shove he pushed Steven over the parapet wall and left him screaming as he plummeted to his inevitable demise forty stories below, taking the soul shredding *reapers* with him.

"No!" yelled Vinchetto. He ran for the edge of the roof and hurled himself over. His wings stayed tight to his side as he dove head first, trying to catch up with Steven. The *reapers* were squealing with anticipation as they clung to their victim and anxiously awaited the chance to tear apart his soul.

Nigel and Natalia saw what was happening and moved with lightening speed to join up with Vinchetto. They both threw themselves off the roof and quickly caught up to Vinchetto. They could see Steven just ahead of them, and he was falling fast.

He was twenty floors down now... nineteen... eighteen, and falling at an unimaginable speed. Vinchetto caught up to him and grabbed him around the waist. Nigel and Natalia pulled at the *reapers*, ripping them from Steven's body as they continued to meet the ground with amazing force.

Vinchetto slowed Steven's fall... sixteen floors... fifteen... slower now, almost to a complete stop. It was if Vinchetto had stopped time all together.

He gently carried Steven's body onto one of the balconies at the twelfth floor. Steven landed on his feet and stood petrified, not understanding what had just happened. It felt as if a powerful gust of wind had caught him around his middle and pushed at him until his fall had come to a halt. This may have been possible, but how did he get onto the balcony?

As he stood there in complete shock, trying to justify any ridiculous explanation as to what happened... he saw them. Vinchetto,

Nigel and Natalia floated in front of him, just outside the balcony twelve floors up. A soft glow of light surrounded them and their wings were open in full glory. One of them spoke to him.

"You have been given a second chance Steven Carvell. Make the most of it." Vinchetto smiled at him and only a moment later the three angels disappeared from his sight and left him standing there... alone.

CHAPTER 20

Steven didn't know what to do now. He was stuck on the balcony of a room that might not be occupied. How would he get out of here? He didn't even know what room this was.

He knocked on the sliding glass door, hoping someone would be there to let him in. The lights came on and a man opened the slider wearing nothing but a pair of bright red boxers. He didn't seem surprised, or even frightened by the fact that there was a man standing on his balcony twelve floors up. But upon further investigation Steven noticed that the man was completely drunk.

"I didn't order any room service," slurred the man in the red boxers.

"Oh, sorry sir, I must have the wrong room. I'll just be going then," Steven quickly moved toward the door and looked back at the drunken man again. "I'm so sorry to have woken you sir."

"Hey don't worry about it, all these rooms look alike," his breath reeked of booze and it escaped every pore in his body. Steven could remember a few nights like that himself. He slipped out the door and shut it quickly behind him. He walked toward the elevator, trying to hurry so he could get some distance between himself and room 1226. He turned the corner and slumped down the wall into a quivering pile of nerves on the floor. He took out his cell phone, hands shaking so hard he could barely dial, and called Katie.

"Katie? Um... can you come and get me?" his voice cracked as he spoke.

"Of course. Are you crying? What happened?" the concern in her voice was evident; there was no sense in hiding it now. It had been a crazy night all the way around for everyone.

"I... was... um... just saved by... angels," he burst into an uncontrollable crying fit. He covered his eyes with his free hand and sobbed.

"We'll be right there," she hung up and Steven sat there for awhile trying to get a hold of himself. He was going to have to do some serious reflecting on his life. He had been given a rare opportunity at a second chance to make things right again. He only hoped that he would be up to that challenge.

It's not so easy for a leopard to change his spots, but there's nothing like a little divine intervention to kick your redemption into high gear.

ζ

Nigel, Natalia and Vinchetto joined the rest of the crew back on the roof. The *soldiers* and *crows* were disappearing in vast numbers and the *higher levels* had all rejoined their precious Prince of Darkness in the rotting abyss of Hell.

This was *not* what Leo had apprised them of during the review of this assignment. They were outmatched when they first arrived and Leo didn't send teams in unprepared without good reason. Nigel would find out what the reason was when he reported back to Leo later on.

It was time for them to return to *Salvation City*. Brad and Sophie had already joined up with them again so they wouldn't have to call them back. They all transported back to their home, a little worse for the wear, but still all in one piece.

None of them could get over what Sarah had done to Nadira. This would become legend in *Salvation City* the instant the news hit. Not to mention the grief that Vinchetto would get for sending out the *call*. He had never done that before, he would have to exaggerate the details in order to maintain his reputation. Hopefully the others would back his story.

As they made their grand entrance into the main hall the entire city boomed with cheers, whistles and applause. From ten floors up in all directions cheering and chanting echoes could be heard repeating over and over again, "Vinchetto… Vinchetto".

Vinchetto looked around the main hall and up at the other floors. He raised his hands to the rambunctious crowd that now surrounded him. He smiled in embarrassment and shouted, "Thank you, thank you… no applause are necessary!" Nigel and Brad just looked at him and laughed.

"You know you'll never live this down, *Vinnie the Bull*," pointed out Brad while he was still sporting a smile at Vinchetto's expense.

"Yeah, yeah... I know," replied Vinchetto as they unloaded their gear in the weapons room.

"Well, don't worry. The spotlight will be off you as soon as word gets around about Sarah and Nadira," said Nigel.

"Me? Why? Don't you guys usually do that to the demons?" asked Sarah, as if her defeat over Nadira was common practice.

"No... we don't," pointed out Natalia. "We can hold them off, but seldom do we send them back to Hell. That was extraordinary!"

"Yeah... you rock chickita!" Joshua always added his own personal flare to a conversation.

"Thanks Joshua," Sarah replied.

"Hey Joshua, where'd you learn to use your swords like that anyway?" asked Nigel.

"What, are you serious? The movies, of course!" he replied while shaking his head in disbelief, as if the shock was about to kill him... again.

"I died before movies and television were invented... remember?" replied Nigel.

"Oh boy, here we go," Calista chimed in.

"I learned how to sword fight from some of the greatest movies ever made! Oh dude, I got to tell you, there's nothing like the movies!" Joshua's enthusiasm boiled over and the entire group watched him with amusement as he rambled on and on. "There's this movie series about these people in space, and they have these special swords made out of lasers... oh, and they have special mind powers too! They travel all around the galaxy fighting this evil emperor and his cool sidekick..."

Nigel whispered to Sarah, "I'm almost sorry I asked now." She laughed and they listened as Joshua continued on with his movie review.

ζ

Usually Nigel would meet with Leo alone after an assignment had been completed, but this time Leo wanted the entire group to be present. Nigel had no doubt it was because of the level of demons present and their lack of warning prior to dispatching.

"I'm sure all of you are wondering why I didn't give you the complete details on Steven Carvell and the demons that would also have an interest in him," Leo said with his commanding presence.

"It crossed our minds," replied Vinchetto.

"It's no secret that while you were alive you were given many trials and tests. You either passed them, or you didn't," he continued. "Well, it's no different here. While every assignment is in essence a test, there will be times when we put you into situations that we know you won't be able to handle. We want to know how you deal with these situations."

"What are you looking for in these tests?" asked Brad.

"Well now, if I tell you that then I may as well hand you the answers to your third period English quiz while I'm at it. But I will say this… this test was specifically for Vinchetto. And you'll be happy to know that he passed."

"Me? But I thought this assignment was for Maggie," replied Vinchetto, a little bit confused.

"Yes, well… sometimes I *divert* the truth for the greater good," Leo explained.

"What was his test?" asked Maggie, but she already knew the answer. They all knew what the answer was. They couldn't spend as much time with each other as they did without knowing most of their friends' personality flaws.

"I wanted to see if Vinchetto would swallow his pride and call for help," Leo smiled at Vinchetto, knowing that he would understand completely. "And he passed with flying colors. Even knowing how much grief he would get from all of you."

The entire room was watching Vinchetto, smiling at their friend with the greatest admiration. They all knew how tough it had to be for him to send out the *call*, but he did it to save the *mortal* and his fellow redeemers.

"Now, I want to address Sarah," Leo moved forward with his agenda. "Sarah, I want to extend my admiration to you for the skill you've already acquired, and more importantly your bravery. You took on Nadira without a second thought, and you sent her back to her *Master* no less. We are all proud of what you have accomplished in the short time you've been here."

"Thank you Leo," she was just so glad that she didn't get hacked to pieces by that horrible demon that she couldn't even think about what an amazing feat she had accomplished.

"You seem to have found your niche'," he replied. "Until next time my angels," Leo's face faded from the hologram.

CHAPTER 21

"So Jason, tell me what's going on with you," the man in the blue sweater vest said to him as he tapped his upper lip with his manicured index finger. Jason found the tapping very irritating.

The man in the blue sweater vest sat in a big, squishy armchair across from Jason's wheelchair in an office full of pictures that had lame sayings like, *Teamwork* and *Courage* captioned below photos of the ocean and Mt. Fuji. It was all so predictable. At any moment he might pull out the giant ink blots and ask Jason what he saw when he looked at them. Ridiculous!

What did Mr. Sweater Vest *think* was going on with him? He killed an entire family, and the sooner everyone realized this the sooner Jason could continue to wallow in his own self-loathing without being bothered. The only reason he even came here today was because his mother wanted him to. What a waste of time... and money.

"Is that a serious question?" Jason replied with disdain. "I *killed* a family, that's what's going on with me," he shook his head and rolled his eyes, refusing to make eye contact with Mr. Sweater Vest.

"You didn't *kill* a family Jason. You were the sole survivor in a fatal car accident... there's a difference," he replied, not allowing Jason's tone to dictate the conversation. Mr. Sweater Vest was quite used to dealing with these kinds of situations and defusing any animosity that goes along with it.

"That's not what the headlines read," Jason countered, he started to bite at his fingernails. He hadn't done this since he was little, and he only did it when he was frustrated or nervous.

"I read the headlines, Jason. A reporter's job is simple...they find ways to exaggerate a situation to sell newspapers... period. You do know that... right?" He continued, "What happened was an accident, it wasn't something you planned."

"Tell that to Sarah Bradley," tears were welling in Jason's eyes at the thought of Sarah's last act of desperation. He watched as

Mr. Sweater Vest wrote something on his notepad and Jason's irritation level elevated.

"You're not responsible for Sarah Bradley. She was a grown woman and made a choice. We always have choices. No matter what happens to us in life we are still ultimately responsible for ourselves and the choices we've made," Mr. Sweater Vest's words of truth fell flat on Jason's ears, his mind was still occupied with events from his past.

He bit at his nails with more aggression now. Why was he so irritated? Maybe if Jason could see the four decaying *crows* that were lingering in Mr. Sweater Vest's office right now he would understand why. Considering their only mission is to stir unrest and despair in their victims, they were clearly accomplishing that mission at an alarming rate.

"It doesn't matter what you say to me, what happened that night was my fault... and what happened to Sarah," said Jason in a low voice, barely louder than a whisper.

"Well, if that's how you truly feel, then you're just going to have to find a way to *forgive* yourself," he continued to write on his notepad. One of the *crows* from Hell was perched on the back of his chair, peering over

Mr. Sweater Vest's shoulder with its yellow eyes as he wrote.

"Not gonna happen," Jason replied sharply.

"Then you'll at least have to find a way to *live* with yourself, if nothing else." Mr. Sweater Vest could feel the anxiety the *crows* emitted off their very being, but he was used to dealing with people in despair and tried to chalk it up to just another patient in pain. But for some reason this time seemed to be different. He couldn't quite put his finger on it, but he could feel the heavy weight they brought to the room. As if there was something inherently evil that was present with them.

"Jason, this is a tough question, but I have to ask you... Have you been having thoughts of suicide?"

Jason squirmed in his wheelchair and tried to give a convincing little half chuckled response. "No... of course not," he lied. He refused to make eye contact; if he had then Mr. Sweater Vest would have seen right through him. Maybe even read his mind... these guys can do that.

"Sorry, but I had to ask. I can't send you home if I know that you're a danger to yourself," he replied and tapped at his upper lip again.

That annoying tapping!

"I'm fine... really. You don't need to worry about me. I don't even have access to drugs or sharp objects. Ask my mom, she'll tell you," he tried to over compensate his reassurance, but Mr. Sweater Vest could read him like a book. He knew that Jason was under real duress, but unless Jason admitted it, or worse, tried to actually hurt himself, his hands were tied. The kid seemed fairly stable. He was clearly torn up over what happened, but he was stable none the less... for now anyway.

"Well, our time is up. But I'd like to see you back here next week," Mr. Sweater Vest rose from his chair and walked toward his desk. The *crow* from Hell that was perched on his chair flew toward the window valance, and another of the diseased, decaying *crows* that had taken up residence on his computer monitor fluttered its wings with unease as he drew closer.

He scribbled something on a piece of paper and handed it to Jason.

"I want you to call me anytime, day or night, if you need anything. If you just want to talk... or whatever just call."

Jason took the piece of paper and put it in his shirt pocket.

"I will, thank you," he replied and he wheeled himself around and faced the door. "You can't tell my mom what we talk about, can you?" he asked.

"Nope, everything we talk about is purely confidential. I can't say a word unless you ask me to," replied Mr. Sweater Vest as he hurried to beat Jason to the door and opened it for him. Jason's mom was sitting in the waiting room and rose when she saw them heading toward her.

"Are you ready honey?" she asked Jason.

"Yeah, can we just go home mom?" he asked. Joanne looked at Mr. Sweater Vest and he nodded at her.

"Sure," she said. They left the office and Mr. Sweater Vest could feel the weight in the room lifting like a dense fog. It appeared for a moment as if the light in the room grew brighter too. He had never experienced anything quite as intense as the despair that followed young Jason Stevens around, but he hoped that somehow he would be able to help him. Time would tell of course.

CHAPTER 22

The atmosphere in *Salvation City* was a bit more somber than usual. The typical busy chatter was nothing more than the low hum of a beehive compared to its usual hustle and bustle. Whispers of Sarah's defeat over Nadira spread throughout the city in monumental proportions, and Vinchetto was still getting nudged every now and then over sending out the *call*.

Nigel, Natalia and Brad decided that their teams needed some much deserved R&R after their assignment in good ole' Sin City. They thought that perhaps a *movie night* would do them some good. The challenge would be deciding what movie everyone could all agree on. This would be fun.

"Listen up everyone," Brad addressed everyone to get their undivided attention. "We have some good news."

"I won the lottery?" asked Vinchetto.

"Yeah, cause you need the money," laughed Maggie.

"I do," countered Vinchetto. "I need a new suit, and maybe some cool new ties like David's."

"I bet if you ask David nicely he'll give you one of his," Calista added. "I think the purple one would look great on you." They all laughed and bantered back and forth amongst each other.

"Hey, do you guys want the good news or not?" hollered Natalia.

"Quiet down everyone," said Sophie, and others joined in to hush those around them.

"What a rowdy bunch," said Brad. "Anyway, we've decided that we're all going to the movies!" Everyone started to clap and cheer. They all loved going down to earth every once in awhile for something other than just the grim work of their assignments. It makes them a little nostalgic to see the life they left behind.

"Rather than go to the movie theater we thought it would be better to go to someone's home and watch a movie," Natalia informed them. They all agreed and nodded at the idea. It would be much more relaxing if they could kick back in the living room of a real home, almost like being back in their own homes again.

"We've chosen a family that's away for a few days, so we'll have the whole house to ourselves," said Nigel.

"Are you ready to go?" asked Brad. They all cheered with overwhelming enthusiasm and followed them to the main hall. Brad, Nigel and Natalia led the pack and the others followed their leaders' energy forces and transported to the same destination.

ζ

They arrived in the family room of a beautiful home with a television screen big enough to put any movie theater to shame. On either side of the TV were floor to ceiling shelves filled with every kind of movie imaginable. There were hundreds, possibly over a thousand DVD's that lined these walls.

"Am I in... Heaven?" asked Joshua as he stared in awe at the entertainment mecca that stood before him.

"Everyone thank Joshua for this brief, yet much deserved, reprieve from our duties of soul salvation," said Nigel with a smile. They all clapped and yelled out their thanks to the young, but not so modest, Joshua as he bowed to the crowd and told them they were very, very welcome.

Joshua turned to the Nigel and asked, "How is it my idea exactly?"

"Well, the way you were carrying on with such enthusiasm about your beloved movies, we thought everyone might enjoy them," explained Nigel. "Besides, we all needed a break."

"Cool!" he replied with a grin.

"Joshua, you want to do the honors of picking out the movie?" asked Brad.

"Oh yeah!" he replied.

"Let me guess… the space movie about the people with the *special mind powers* and the *laser light swords*," stated Vinchetto with a tone that pointed out the obvious. He smiled at Joshua's excitement over the chance to share his lifelong movie passion.

"Is that ok with everyone?" Joshua asked.

"Of course it is, are you kidding!" claimed Calista. They all shouted in approval at his movie choice and Joshua's grin widened with all the excitement of a child.

"Come on, let's watch a movie already," hollered Samuel.

The family dog had wandered into the room only to find it filled with angels. His tail wagged with lightening speed and he barked in excitement at his welcome houseguests.

"Hey there boy," said Sarah and she bent down to shower the dog with affection. He quickly dropped to the floor and rolled onto his back inviting some serious and well deserved belly scratches. Chloe, from Brad's team, sat on the floor next to Sarah and the dog and joined in the belly rub duty.

It was nice to be seen for who they really were and to be accepted without fear or doubt. Animals are as pure and innocent as small children, trust and love are all they know how to give. It's in the very core of their nature, and they have yet to ever be tainted by discrimination and hate.

As Natalia worked on starting the DVD player and the TV, with the help of Joshua of course, the family cat wandered in to see what all the commotion was about. She purred as loud as an outboard motor as she wrapped and twined herself around Natalia's leg in affection. The cat looked up at her visitor and jumped into the unsuspecting arms of Natalia.

This hardcore warrior of redeeming souls was suddenly softened by the cuddly, fluffy affection of this little orange and white, purring feline. The cat looked up at Natalia with her green eyes and meowed.

"Well, hello there kitty," said Natalia. "What's your name?" The cat continued to purr and nuzzled herself deeper into Natalia's arms. She managed to get the movie playing while holding her newfound friend and the TV burst into life; complete with surround sound and a colorful brilliance. The crowd cheered and clapped as they settled down to watch one of the best movies ever made... according to Joshua.

"Calista," whispered Sarah, as the opening credits rolled and the orchestra blared out of the monstrous speakers.

"Yeah Sarah?" she whispered in reply.

"What's the deal with Vinchetto and Arzulu?" Sarah asked. It hadn't escaped her notice that Arzulu conveniently appears at all of Vinchetto's assignments.

"It goes way back to when Vinchetto was still alive," she explained. "The way I hear it, Arzulu was assigned to Vinchetto while he was still in the mortal world. It was Arzulu that influenced Vinchetto to do all those bad things while he worked for the mob."

"Well, I can see why Vinchetto is so determined not to let Arzulu get the best of him now." Sarah put the pieces together and understood the *real* reason why Vinchetto didn't want to cross over into Heaven. Although he had earned his redemption, he still had unfinished business to take care of. Just like so many others that still remained in *Salvation City*. Everyone finds their redemption in their own time... sometimes after they've already earned it.

Sarah wondered if she too would choose to stay after she earned the right to be with her family again. She would have to cross that bridge when she reached it. For now she just wanted to enjoy the friendships she'd made and the meaningful work she was doing for the lost souls out there that were just like her.

"Pipe down everyone," said Vinchetto. "The movie's starting already... geez louize you're a noisy bunch!" The crowd booed him and he hunched over as if ducking hurling objects. They all laughed and finally settled in to watch the movie and spend some rare, peaceful time together. All seemed right with the universe... for the moment. But as they knew all too well, peace is fleeting and work would soon be upon them again.

CHAPTER 23

Jason took the pill out of his mouth after his mother left the room and wheeled himself over to his desk. He carefully popped open the side of his computer hard drive and took out a plastic baggy that was now stuffed with pills that he had hidden there.

They were all different, prescribed to Jason for different levels and pain and sleep deprivation. He had quite the stash piled up; if he ever decided to take up a career as a drug dealer he would have a hefty inventory to start with.

He looked around the room and quickly added the pill he took out of his cheek to the baggy. He replaced the secret stash, closed up the panel on the side of his computer and wheeled himself over to his bed.

Wheelchair bound or not, he still managed to do a few things for himself, like hurling himself out of his chair and into his bed. His mom would be in soon to make sure he hadn't fallen flat on his face in the process.

He couldn't remember when he had actually made the conscious decision to start saving up his pills to take all at once. Something inside him seemed to be driving him to do it. He was constantly angry and irritated too, which wasn't like him at all. It seems to have all started just after Sarah Bradley killed herself. Everything completely spiraled out of control after he was given that horrible piece of news.

Slowly, but surely, Jason seemed to be slipping into a continuous state of hate and despair. Guilt was now his only driving force and it consumed every inch of him. It penetrated every thought and feeling he had at all times. This was not who he was, but he couldn't stop the out of control freight train that was now his life.

Little did Jason know, he had constant companions that pushed these horrible feelings of guilt, hate and despair into the very heart of him. They lingered in his presence at all times, drowning him with doubt and pain.

He'd tried many times to explain the feelings he was having to his mom, but something stopped him every time he opened his mouth. It almost felt as if an invisible force shoved his jaw closed the moment his would-be confessions bubbled to the surface of his conscience.

He didn't know what was wrong with him, but he knew he couldn't take it anymore. Jason Stevens wanted to die, and he was bound and determined to do that very thing. But when... that was something he hadn't quite decided just yet. He should have enough pills to do the job effectively, but there was a little, small voice in his head that kept him from taking that plunge into the ultimate finality.

He leaned over toward his nightstand and pushed aside his alarm clock. Jason had tucked away a piece of paper beneath the clock, where it couldn't be seen by any prying eyes. He tugged at the corner of the paper and it came free from its hiding place. He unfolded it and looked at the phone number that was written there.

call anytime

452-9843

Mr. Sweater Vest, or should he call him *Dr. Sweater Vest*, had given Jason his personal number in case he ever needed to talk.

His real name, of course, wasn't *Mr. Sweater Vest*, it was Dr. Jeremy Cavanaugh. Although Jason didn't necessarily share the same wardrobe styles as Dr. Cavanaugh, he did seem to genuinely care about Jason and his emotional well-being. But more importantly, he would understand the turmoil that Jason was suffering through right now.

Jason couldn't understand why he had shut down in Dr. Cavanaugh's office the other day, but it felt like something inside him had seized control again. All he could feel was anger and resentment, and it wasn't allowing him to talk about what was really happening to him. The same way it takes over when he tries to talk to his mom, almost as if something is physically controlling his actions.

There were three quick raps at his bedroom door and then it started to open. Jason quickly slid the paper with Dr. Cavanaugh's number under his covers. His dad came in tonight instead of his mom, he must want to discuss something.

"Hey there kiddo," said his dad in a soft voice. "How are you feeling tonight?"

"Fine," Jason replied looking down at his hands when he answered his father.

"I invited the pastor from the church over tonight," he sat on the bed next to his son. "I've asked him to come over and give you a blessing. He brought Mr. Barney and Mr. Andrews with him."

"Dad...," Jason couldn't complete his sentence before his father interrupted.

"Don't say no... you need this more than you think you do," he paused and sighed. "I need it too. Ok?" insisted his father, he was holding Jason's hand.

"Ok," Jason looked into his father's eyes and squeezed his hand tight. His father smiled at him, rose from the bed and headed for the door.

He returned a few moments later with Pastor Richards and the two other men from church trailing close behind. Jason's room wasn't very big, but the four men managed to fit around his bed, two on each side, with room to spare. They rested their hands on Jason's head and Pastor Richards started to pray for this tormented soul that lay helpless in front of them.

"Our most dear and gracious Heavenly Father, we ask that you be with Jason David

Stevens... guiding and comforting him through this terrible trial which he has had to endure...," his prayer went on and Jason could feel the weight lifting off his body. He felt almost euphoric as the pastor continued; it was as if he was submerged in warm, gently moving water.

His mind and body floated somewhere between time and space, as he imagined the darkness that had so long surrounded him being erased by the calming light of the Spirit. For the first time in months Jason felt like he could breathe, like his heart was actually beating again. His eyes were closed, but he could feel the warm, salty tears running down his cheeks.

Relief... warmth... love. That's what he felt right now.

The *crows*, which had become a permanent fixture in the life of Jason Stevens, were cawing and flying frantically around the room as if it were a blazing inferno. There were more than a dozen by this time and they had been quite busy raining down their anxiety and pain on Jason.

But now the *crows* were completely helpless. All their hard work for the past few weeks had been for nothing. A blinding light now surrounded Jason that couldn't be penetrated no matter how hard they flew at him screeching and clawing. They flew into each other, scrambling to break through the barrier, but their efforts were useless.

The prayer continued, as if the pastor knew that his work wasn't complete until the *crows* were totally abolished. One by one, they flew into the light like suicide bombers until the light finally annihilated them. Reducing them to nothing more than a faint hint of dissipating dust, they were gone.

There was no doubt that they would return... and with friends. But for the moment Jason Stevens could find a little reprieve from the aching, gut-wrenching guilt that had defined his very existence for the past few weeks. A few weeks that felt like an eternity to this young boy.

Pastor Richards finished with the blessing and the four men stepped back from Jason, looked at him and were completely speechless. They could feel the atmosphere in the room change. An unseen burden had been lifted that night that none of the men would ever be able to explain with words.

They each looked at each other, not quite sure just what to say. Pastor Richards broke the silence.

"How do you feel Jason?" he asked the young boy who was actually smiling for the first time in quite awhile.

"I, uh... actually feel," he stopped for a moment, trying to find the right word to describe what he was feeling, "...relieved." Jason smiled.

"Relieved is good," said Mr. Andrews smiling and patting him on his shoulder.

"I could stand a little relief myself," Mr. Barney added.

"I want to thank you all for coming tonight," said Jason's dad. "I can't explain how much you've just done for our family."

"It was our pleasure... truly," responded Pastor Richards. The three men all shook hands with Jason and his father before they started to make their way out of the small bedroom. Jason's dad was following them out of the room when Jason called to him.

"Dad."

"Yes son?"

"Thank you," Jason smiled at him.

"I love you son... I hope you know that."

"I love you too dad." Jason's dad nodded his head and smiled as he followed his guests out.

Jason could feel the difference the blessing had made in him. His feelings of anger and irritation were completely gone. Although he was still in pain over the accident and Sarah Bradley's death, he at least felt like himself again. He knew that his guilt and pain would never go away, but he couldn't live with the hate that had confiscated his mind for the past few weeks.

Jason closed his eyes and let a peaceful sleep overtake him.

CHAPTER 24

Feeling rejuvenated, Sarah and Vinchetto were on the tenth floor sparring. This had become their favorite pastime and they were paired up pretty evenly. Sarah seemed to get the best of Vinchetto most of the time, however she had a sneaking suspicion that he let her win. Either way, they were seriously honing their skills for the battlefield.

"So, what were those… things that were crawling all over Steven Carvell?" asked Sarah.

"Oh, you mean the *reapers*?" he asked and then continued. "Nasty beasts, ain't they?"

"How come they weren't at the Grayson assignment?"

"Because they're strictly *soul harvesters*," he answered.

"Well, isn't that what all the demons do?" she asked, confused by the roles that some demons had over others.

"No, most are just there to influence people to do things," he explained. "*Soul harvesters* are there for just that... to take souls to Hell."

"Was that because they were extremely bad during their life?"

"Exactly!"

"I get it," she said. "Can I ask you a question?"

"Anything Sarah, you know that," he replied casually.

"Did you have these *reapers* around you when you were dying?"

"I didn't see them, but there's no doubt in my mind that they were there," he paused for a moment, imagining their foul, twisting bodies wrapping around him. He shivered at the thought.

"How come they didn't take you to Hell?"

"Well, when I was killed it wasn't quick and painless, if you know what I mean," he continued. "I had plenty of time to reflect on the things I'd done and the sins I'd committed. So, as I lay there, waiting for death to take me... begging for it really, I asked for God's forgiveness."

"And He forgave you?" she asked, almost surprised.

"Of course, I'm here ain't I?" he replied. "I still had to earn my way into Heaven though. My redemption came with some strings attached, that's how I came to be here, in *Salvation City*."

"I get it... and I'm glad you're here," she said.

"Yeah... me too," Vinchetto smiled and then he made a move at her with his sword that threw hers at least ten feet away from where they were sparring. "I win!"

"I didn't see that coming," she ran over to retrieve her sword.

"That's because I distracted you with my smooth talk,"

"Whatever!" she laughed. "You wish!"

Nigel came up to the tenth floor to find them. He needed to have a team meeting about an assignment that was coming up. An assignment for Sarah to be exact. This one was a big deal for Sarah and it couldn't be given to anyone else, although he was confident that Sarah could handle anything.

ζ

In their gathering room they all sat with silent reverence as they waited for Nigel to tell them what was going on. He looked at Sarah as if he wasn't quite sure how to tell her what this was about.

"As you all know, Leo gives us assignments that are sometimes specifically for someone in the group," he continued. "We never know when we're going to get our own assignment and sometimes it comes much sooner than we expect."

They all looked around at each other, wondering who was up for an assignment. There were still three in the group who hadn't earned their redemption yet, and it could have easily been for any one of them.

"Sarah, I'm sure you've probably guessed, the assignment coming up is for you," revealed Nigel.

"Me?" she asked. "I have no one left in my life that would be impacted by me if I saved them." They all looked at her.

"Are you sure about that?" asked Maggie.

"Yes," she said, and then added, "Well, my mother's still alive. It could be her."

"No," said Nigel. "I'm sure you're not expecting this one."

"Who is it?" she asked.

"Jason Stevens is going to kill himself Sarah," answered Nigel.

All the color drained from Sarah's face as she quickly remembered the depth of his sorrow when he had visited the family gravesite. She knew he was hurting, but she hadn't realized that he was in such an irreversible state of despair.

"When?" she asked, her voice cracked as she spoke.

"Soon, Leo will call on us any time now," informed Nigel. "You can have any of us go with you if you like."

"Can I have all of you go with me?" she asked as she looked around the room at her team... her family.

"You bet we'll be there!" claimed Calista. There was no way she would leave Sarah on her own, even though Sarah was clearly able to handle herself in a fight. Everyone in the room agreed and reassured her that they would be with her for this assignment. Relief washed over her pale face and she tried to mentally prepare herself to save the person that took away her only reasons to live.

She was completely torn with conflicting emotions. She hadn't felt this way since she was still alive. Although she knew that Jason was just an innocent kid, his life completely changed by the accident too, she couldn't let go of the pain he had caused her. Her death was of her own doing, and she understood that, but she couldn't help but believe that he was somewhat responsible for her.

If he hadn't killed Will and Joey, she'd still be alive. That was a fact, plain and simple. She could go crazy trying to sort out the emotions that were running through her right now, but she needed to pull herself together and do what was right.

"Ok," she replied to everyone. "I guess I'll have to be ready."

CHAPTER 25

After Jason's blessing he felt fine... for awhile at least. But it didn't take long for his faithful companions to regroup and make his life Hell again. This time they brought re-enforcements with them. Besides the decaying *crows* of unrest and despair, the Prince of Darkness sent eight *soldiers* along on this mission. Apparently he grew tired of waiting... patience was for the weak, not for him and his powerful reign of terror.

Soon the *angels of redemption* would be sent to save this *mortal* and intervene in any acts of desperation Jason might attempt. This would force Satan's hand and he would have no choice but to send in a *higher level...* or two... to seal the deal. Even if he didn't get to keep these desperate souls, it was still fun to push them over the proverbial edge. Satan's personal entertainment, if you will.

The rotting, black *crows* were perched throughout Jason's room, cawing and flapping their decaying wings. They showered Jason with anxiety and uneasiness. The *soldiers* kept fairly quiet for now, slinking around the floor and watching their prey with their terrifying red eyes. They would hiss and screech occasionally, making Jason jump for no apparent reason. It sent cold shivers down his spine.

One of the *soldiers* crawled over to Jason's wheelchair and clawed its way up the side of the chair and across the back of it. It sniffed every inch of Jason as it slinked across the chair, black saliva dripping from its jagged, razor sharp teeth. The anticipation of tormenting this victim was growing more intense among Satan's army with each passing second.

Jason was looking through his scrapbook. He had added Sarah's obituary along with Will's and Joey's. Sarah didn't have a big article in the paper about her death. She died quietly and alone, no fanfare or media coverage to exaggerate the ordinary life that was taken away from her so prematurely. She died just as she had lived during her last three months, completely isolated from the revolving world around her. Sarah was forgotten by everyone... except Jason Stevens.

He lived and breathed *Sarah Bradley*. Every act, every thought, every dream Jason had revolved around Sarah and her family. Jason's conscience and unconscious mind was devoured by his guilt over her death. And soon he would die thinking about Sarah... begging for her forgiveness.

Jason closed the scrapbook, keeping it close to his chest as he wheeled himself over to his desk. He popped open the side of his hard drive, taking out the bag full of pills... the bag that held his demise.

Jason didn't understand that taking these pills would merely be a respite from the daunting internal pain he suffered. He could never escape what he had done, or the constant pain he was in. Suicide was not his atonement for Sarah's death like he believed; it was his eternal punishment for it.

Jason rolled the pills in the bag around in his fingers, feeling the different sizes and shapes. These tiny things held so much power, life... escape from pain... death. The pills themselves were so innocent; it was that hands that held them that decided their true intentions. So many thoughts and emotions raged through Jason, completely out of control as they whirled through his head.

He sat there motionless, still holding his scrapbook and the bag full of pills as he contemplated his next move. Unaware that his new friends had become completely agitated by the pills, Jason could only sense the ceaseless push for him to swallow them. A desire to take them that wasn't his own, but controlled him none the less.

ζ

"Are you ready for this Sarah?" asked Nigel.

"I have to be," she replied. The team was in the weapons room loading up for the onslaught of demons they were sure to encounter in the bedroom of Jason Stevens. They were all silent as they geared up. This was out of the norm for this crew, but they knew what was at stake for Sarah... and for this young, tormented boy.

"Let's go angels!" shouted Nigel. They filed out in perfect formation, as usual, into the main hall and transported themselves to Jason's salvation.

Each of them arrived with a brilliant flash of light into Jason's presence, Vinchetto leading the way. Satan had already taken it upon himself to assume that there would be an entire team of *redemption angels* to save this kid. He had sent in two *higher levels*, including Nadira. And she clearly had a score to settle with Sarah.

Nadira wasted no time drawing her weapon and headed straight for Sarah. Nigel saw her coming and jumped in front of Sarah with his sword drawn.

"Sarah, Jason's all yours, we'll handle the demons," yelled Nigel. His voice was drowned out by the ear rupturing cawing and screeching of the *crows* and the *soldiers*.

"Got it!" she replied and ran over to the boy backed into the corner of his room with his face buried in his hands. The scrapbook and the bag of pills were still sitting in his lap.

There were two of the vile *soldiers* crawling all over Jason, and they screeched with delight in anticipation of his soon-to-be demise. Their sharp talons clawed his chair and dug into his shoulder as Jason remained hunched over, crying into his hands.

A feeling of complete dread and darkness overwhelmed the unsuspecting boy as his tormentors gained ground by raining down on him all the pain and despair they could muster.

Sarah had both swords drawn when she reached Jason, and with almost no effort at all she sliced through the wretched bodies of the *soldiers*. They vanished from Jason's presence, leaving behind only the black smoke residue of their foul existence.

The decaying, black carcasses of the *crows* that were hovering above him cawed and screeched in protest as their accomplices were taken out. They swooped down at Sarah, claws and beaks ready to kill, and without blinking an eye she sent them back to Hell as easily as she had the *soldiers*.

Although the room behind her was still in complete chaos, Sarah had at least freed Jason of the beasts that had been penetrating his mind so intimately. She dropped to her knees in front of him and put her hands on his. He moved his hands from his face and raised his head, his eyes swollen from crying and his cheeks still wet with flowing tears. He clutched at the scrapbook in his lap.

"Oh Jason," said Sarah. "What are you thinking? I can't come back because you kill yourself. This won't change anything!"

He couldn't hear her, or feel her hands on his. He just stared off into the distance, his mind completely overwhelmed with confusion. His parents were gone and wouldn't be back for some time, if he was going to do this it was now or never.

Jason slowly wheeled himself over to his nightstand where his mom had left him a sandwich and a drink, just in case he got hungry while they were out. She took such great care of Jason; everything she did for him was smothered with a mother's love. She wasn't going to take this well. Her entire life revolved around taking care of his every need.

All the more reason for him to swallow those pills. It wasn't fair to his parents; they should be enjoying their life right now, not babying their grown son. No... it wasn't right. He had to do this... and do it now!

Sarah stayed with Jason every inch of the way. She whispered in his ear, persuading him to live.

"Jason," she whispered. "This is Sarah, and I'm telling you that you're not going to do this. You're going to live because you deserve to live."

Jason stopped just short of his nightstand and sat perfectly still. The room was completely silent to Jason's ears, but the commotion going on in the other worldly plane was so loud that the angels could barely hear each other.

The gagging stench of sulfur had already choked out the air and the light was drawing dimmer by the minute as the angels sent the foul *soldiers* and *crows* back to their maker. The two *higher levels* were engaged in full battle with Vinchetto and Nigel, while Calista's and Maggie's task was to keep the *soldiers* and *crows* at bay long enough for Sarah to save this kid. Maggie's guns and Calista's crossbow were quite effective on them, so they were keeping the score pretty even.

"Maggie!" yelled Nigel. "You're going to need to get to Jason's parents. Tell them to come home right now."

"I'm on my way," replied Maggie and she disappeared with a flash of light. Calista would soon be in over her head with all the nasty *crows* and *soldiers* that were still flying around the room. Until the *higher levels* were gone Satan's minions would continue to regenerate their numbers as fast as the redeemers could send them back to Hell.

Despite the chaos that had been unleashed in the room around her, Sarah's only focus was Jason. She didn't know if there was anything she could say that would turn him around. He was in the same state of mind that she was in before she reached the point of no return.

CHAPTER 26

Jason's parents were driving in their SUV when their unseen visitor appeared with ninja stealth into the backseat. Maggie leaned over the front seat, just as she remembers doing as a child, and eavesdropped on their conversation.

"He seems better than he has in awhile," said Bill, Jason's father.

"You think so?" asked Joanne. "I'm not so sure. I think he *wants* us to think he's doing better."

"Maybe," he said. "I know he feels guilty about being a burden on us."

"It doesn't matter what we say to him, he just doesn't get it," Joanne was at her wits end, always trying to make Jason understand that they care for him because they love him, not because they have to.

"I know honey, but what can we do that we're not already doing?"

"I don't know. Only he can change the way he sees things," she stared out the window, totally lost in her thoughts. "If only he would realize that we would go the ends of the earth for him."

Maggie leaned into the front and started talking to her unsuspecting companions.

"You need to turn around right now and go home," said Maggie. "Jason is in trouble and needs your help right away!" She put her hand on Joanne's shoulder. She whispered in her ear, telling her things only a mother would understand.

"Your baby needs you... don't let him down," she continued with her subtle prodding. "Turn the car around and run to your son. If you don't, He... Will... Die." Maggie's tone remained as soft as a whisper, but her words were delivered with a brute force.

"Bill, turn the car around," urged Joanne as she turned to her husband.

"What? Why?" he asked, confused by the sudden panic in her tone.

"Just do it... please!" she looked at her husband and the expression on her face scared him.

"What's wrong?" he asked as he pulled into the turning lane so he could head back home.

"I don't know... I have this horrible feeling in my stomach that something is wrong with Jason."

"Good... now step on it Bill!" said Maggie, her tone was no longer a whisper.

"Call him, it could be awhile before we make it home," he replied. Joanne already had her cell phone out and was dialing the house phone. Jason refused to own a cell phone after the accident; the house phone had become his own private number. He figured that if someone couldn't reach him there, then it wasn't that important in the first place.

Joanne called the house phone, but it went straight to voicemail. She called again... no answer.

"He's not answering?" Bill asked her. He was starting to worry now too.

"No. I hope he didn't turn that stupid ringer off again," she replied as she continued unsuccessfully to reach her son on the phone.

Bill accelerated and pushed their bulky SUV down the surface streets, weaving in and out of traffic as he sped along the busy road. He didn't normally play into Joanne's overprotective, motherly instincts, but oddly enough he was having the same gut feeling that something was wrong.

"Do you have Cammie's number in your phone?" Bill asked Joanne.

"Oh no... why don't I have the neighbors' numbers programmed in my phone?" she was so angry at herself for not thinking ahead and being more prepared in an emergency. If there even was an emergency. But you never know; she should always be prepared.

"Ok, don't worry. I'm sure everything is fine," he reached over and put his hand on her shoulder. "You'll see... he's probably in his room playing those video games of his."

"You're probably right," she turned her head to look out the window. "Let's just get home anyway."

"We're almost there babe," he replied and continued to try and break the sound barrier with his two ton vehicle on a four lane side street. He sure hoped there were no cops around, but little did he know there was an angel looking out for their safe return home right now. A speeding ticket was the least of their worries.

CHAPTER 27

Jason continued to roll the pills around in his hand. He dumped them all onto his bed and counted them. One, two, three... forty-two... fifty-seven pills in all. Yep, that should do the trick.

"No!" yelled Sarah. "You're not going to take those... I forbid it!" she was in his face, clutching it with both of her hands.

The chaos in the room grew more intense as Jason drew closer to his final decision. Calista was having a hard time holding back the minions of Hell. For every vile beast she vanquished it seemed that two returned in their place. Nigel and Vinchetto kept up their vigilant fight against the *higher levels*, as their swords whipped through the air with the speed of light.

Arzulu wasn't present here, so Vinchetto was actually having an easier time than he anticipated. Nigel, however, was struggling to hold back Nadira. She continued to drive forward, pushing Nigel back and back. She wanted Sarah so badly, and the only way to get at her would be to break through Nigel.

Nadira had driven Nigel back into a corner and continued to beat down on his sword with hers. Faster and harder her sword cracked against his, until all he could do was hold his sword out in front of him and take the blows. Her anger and hatred pushing her into an unrelenting state of madness. Black spittle flew from her clenched teeth as she screamed in anger with every blow to Nigel's sword.

The force of Nadira's violence was more than Nigel could withstand. He found himself slipping down the wall, hunching in the corner while he kept his sword raised out in front of him to hold back the onslaught of Nadira's frenzied rage.

"Vinchetto!" hollered Nigel.

"I'm coming brother!" he replied without hesitation. Vinchetto kicked his demon in the chest and knocked him onto the floor. Vinchetto rushed over to his fallen opponent and raised his sword above his head. He gritted his teeth together, and with a loud grunt of rage he forced his sword downward, impaling his weakened adversary.

With a deafening scream of tormented pain, the demon grabbed at the sword that penetrated his wretched, evil body. Vinchetto pulled his sword out and with one swift motion he raised it up again and swung it sideways, taking off the demon's head. He disappeared in a blaze of shame and a swirling tornado of black smoke.

Vinchetto wasted to time rushing to Nigel's defense. Nadira, however would not be taken by surprised and turned toward Vinchetto just before he reached her. She slashed her sword across his chest as he rushed forward and stopped him dead in his tracks. He looked down at his chest and saw the pure white light that bled from his gaping wound. He staggered back and dropped to the floor. Nigel, still slumped in the corner, yelled to his friend as he tried to pull himself up from the floor.

Nadira wasted no time heading for her intended prey... Sarah. She raised her sword out to her side in preparation of a sharp, quick swing toward Sarah's neck. Calista, watching the events unfold as she struggled with her own demons, screamed at Nadira in protest of her intended move.

"No!" screamed Calista again as she threw herself through the air, directly into the path of Nadira's swinging sword. As the sword cut across the air it connected with Calista's shoulder and sliced her completely in half. A pure, blinding, white light burst out of Calista's severed body and filled the room. The pure energy that spilled from Calista annihilated the *soldiers* and the *crows* that were caught in its path. A moment later there was an incredible burst of blinding whiteness, and then the light was gone... and so was Calista.

"Oh no! No, no, no!" screamed Sarah. "This can't be happening... not for me!" she cried in protest. Sarah lost her control over Jason in her disbelief of Calista's fate, and in the brief seconds that passed he scooped up a handful of pills and tossed them in his mouth.

Sarah wasn't aware of what Jason had done; she was too focused on Nadira. Sarah rushed at Nadira with her swords and began bombarding her with the same raging blows that Nadira had unleashed on Nigel.

Vinchetto still lay on the floor, clutching at his chest as the light slowly seeped from his wound. Nigel regained himself and joined in Sarah's battle to finish off this horrid, evil spawn of Satan.

Jason, left to his own devices, continued to swallow the remainder of the fifty-seven pills that he had so carefully counted. It was only when he had taken the last of them that Sarah had realized what had happened. She left Nadira to Nigel and rushed back over to this poor young man, whose fate was now sealed... thanks to her selfishness.

"No Jason," she begged him. "Please... throw it up!" she cried as she knelt down in front of him and stroked his face. "Please, baby... please! It's not over yet, get it out... throw it up!" she commanded him. But he wasn't responding to her, his eyes were growing heavy and his skin looked pale. She had to do something right now... but what?

"Sarah!" yelled Vinchetto. She looked over at him, feeling completely helpless to save Jason.

"What should I do?" she asked in a desperate voice.

"Show yourself to him," he answered.

"How?" she asked.

"You have to *will* it," he replied. "You can do it Sarah, I know you can."

She turned back toward Jason and closed her eyes. With everything she had inside her, every thought, every wish, with every dream she had ever desired she *willed* herself to be seen.

ζ

Jason sat there in disbelief as the light that appeared before him grew brighter and brighter... and even brighter still. At first he thought it was the drugs, merely a hallucination, but as the light grew brighter it began to take the form of a person.

Sarah... he thought to himself.

Slowly the light began to subside, and as clear as day Sarah Bradley kneeled before him. He couldn't believe his eyes... this couldn't be happening! But it had to be, there she was, right in front of him.

She spoke.

"Jason," she said to him.

"Are... are you real?" he asked.

"Yes," she answered. "I have to tell you something very important." He just stared at her, confused and feeling numb from all the drugs.

"Jason, I want you to know that I forgive you... and I love you." Tears that sparkled like diamonds escaped her angelic eyes. Jason burst into an uncontrollable crying fit, this angel before him was actually forgiving him for the atrocity that he had committed against her. He didn't deserve to be forgiven for what he had done.

"Let it go Jason. Don't give up on yourself," she continued. "You deserve to grow up and have a family of your own someday. I did this to myself, you didn't kill me." She confessed her mistake to this tormented soul.

The decaying, black *crows* from Hell, along with their vile companions, the *soldiers,* all continued to flap around the room anxiously. Just waiting for the pills to take this poor kid to his doom. This wasn't over for them, not by a long shot. Nadira and Nigel continued to fight; the clashing of their swords still filled this small room with the maddening sound of metal against metal.

Sarah looked around at the mayhem that surrounded her and Jason. His time was running out quickly, he took a lot of pills and he was very thin and frail. It wouldn't take long for the pills to snatch the life out of him.

"Jason," she commanded. "I need you to stay with me now! Pick up the phone," she instructed. Jason's eyes were closing and everything was starting to blur. He reached for the phone; his arm felt like it weighed a thousand pounds. It dropped to his side again.

"Come on Jason!" she yelled. "You can do it!" He picked up his heavy arm again and struggled to grab the phone. It was hard to grab, there were so many phones and they kept moving, but finally Jason was able to grab a hold of it.

"Good boy... now dial 9-1-1," Sarah told him. The numbers were just a blur. He moved the phone closer to his face in an attempt to focus better. He tried to dial. 9... 1... almost done, just one more number... 1. He set the phone down as it connected to the operator. Sarah could faintly hear the muffled voice through the earpiece that lay in Jason's lap, *"9-1-1, what's your emergency?"*

Oh thank God, Sarah thought to herself. They would be on the scene soon, even if Jason didn't speak to them. She would stay with him, letting herself be seen until the paramedics arrived.

Sarah took a look around at the devastation that was unfolding in this small bedroom. Time itself seemed to slow as she watched the chaos escalate into a state of boundless contention between good and evil.

Vinchetto was hurt so bad that he couldn't move. Nigel was still struggling with Nadira. The *crows* and *soldiers* of Hell were flying out of control around the room, waiting for the inevitable demise of young Jason Stevens. All control was lost… if it ever existed at all.

And Calista… poor Calista, she was gone. She had sacrificed herself for Sarah. Why would she do that? Sarah couldn't think about that now, her mission was to save this young boy. And she wouldn't fail… she couldn't fail.

CHAPTER 28

"Oh... my... God! Bill!" screamed out Joanne in a sheer panic.

"I know!" he replied. They screeched into the driveway, barely stopping before hitting the garage door. A paramedic, two police cars and a fire truck were parked in a haphazard fashion in front of the house. Blue and red lights twirled with intimidation, bouncing off the surrounding houses and lighting up the neighborhood. People from up and down the street had come out of their homes to see what all the commotion was about... looky-loos, and nothing more.

Joanne was getting out of the SUV before Bill had even come to a complete stop and bolted for the front door. Before she could even enter the house the paramedics were wheeling Jason out, strapped to a gurney with an oxygen mask over his face. The repugnant stench of vomit hit her square in the face before she could even see it covering the front of her son.

She couldn't tell if he was conscious or not, but his head seemed to be lolling back and forth on the gurney. He must be alive, at least he wasn't being taken out in a body bag. *Why did we leave him alone?* She scolded herself.

"How's my son?" she asked the paramedics that were wheeling him to their van for transport.

"He'll be fine, ma'am," one of them replied. "He's going to have one hell of a sore throat for awhile, but he'll make it."

"Oh thank God," she clutched at her chest and started to cry. Bill came up behind her and grabbed her shoulders, as if to steady her.

Two police officers came out of the house behind the paramedics and the fire department. Joanne and Bill could hear the police chatter coming from their radios and one of the officers responded. They were speaking in their police banter, so they couldn't understand what their response actually was.

One of the officers approached the couple.

"Are you Mr. and Mrs. Stevens?" she asked them.

"Yes," they answered in unison.

"Your son is a very lucky young man," she continued. "If we had gotten here just a minute later we may not have been able to save him. He definitely had an angel watching over him tonight."

Joanne sighed and closed her eyes. She felt so weak that she was sure she might actually pass out. This was the same feeling she had the night the police came to the door to inform them of Jason's car accident. They both hoped they would never have to experience anything like that ever again... yet here they were.

"Where did he get all those pills?" the second officer asked.

"I don't know sir," Bill responded. "We control his medication; he doesn't even have access to it."

"Well, he could have been storing them up. Making you think he was taking them when he actually wasn't," he replied. "We've seen this kind of thing before."

A third officer came up behind them from inside the house. He had a wet towel that he was using in an attempt to wash the vomit from his sleeve. The third officer was a huge, burly guy that looked like he was straight out of an old western movie.

"Sorry about the towel folks," he apologized as he handed the vomit covered towel to Joanne. "But I had to do what I had to do."

"You made him throw up?" Bill asked.

"Yeah," he said casually. "I didn't see any other options." Joanne started to cry and hugged the big, burly officer. He hugged her back and the other two officers just stared at him.

"You saved my son," she choked out the words with a cracking voice.

"They're taking him to the County Hospital," said one of the other officers. "You can meet them there. We'll take some statements from both of you and your son when he's stable."

"Thank you officers," said Bill, he had been overcome with emotion as well and found it hard to spit out just a few simple words.

"Alright then," said the big, burly officer. "We'll see you there."

The three officers got into the two cars and turned off their lights. The paramedic van had pulled out and was heading to the hospital, lights still rolling, but no sound effects from the siren. The fire department loaded up as well and headed back to the station house, leaving Bill and Joanne standing there... alone.

They looked at each other, locked up the house and got back into their vehicle, not a breath of a word between them. After they got into the SUV and headed toward the hospital, they looked over at each other and held each other's hands... still in complete silence.

CHAPTER 29

Jason's throat felt like it had been flushed out with drain cleaner, it was excruciating! And what was that horrible taste? It tasted... and felt... like he had eaten an entire bag of charcoal briquettes. Without any water!

"Well, hello there!" said a cheerful voice. Jason struggled to open his eyes, his lids felt like they had been sewn shut. His throat was on fire and when he swallowed it felt completely swollen.

"Here," said the cheerful voice, Jason could almost see her now. She had a round face with rosy cheeks and her scrubs had some colorful pattern that he couldn't quite get into focus yet. She helped him sit up and spoon fed him some ice chips from a foam cup.

Cats! That was the pattern on her scrubs... cats! He could see more clearly now. He tried to talk, but nothing came out and it made his throat ache even worse.

"Don't try to talk," she scolded. "Give your throat a rest. You were doing quite the exorcist impression a couple of hours ago." She smiled at him and handed him the cup of ice and the spoon.

"Just a little at a time, ok?" He nodded in agreement. She smiled and left him alone in his emergency room station. He struggled to sit up more and when he did, he saw someone sitting in a chair by the nurse's station. He was still having a hard time focusing, but eventually the figure became quite clear.

It was Sarah.

She had stayed with him the entire time. She still allowed herself to be seen by Jason, but no one else had any clue to her presence. When she saw that he had noticed her, she got up and walked over to him.

"Hi," she said to him, smiling. A faint glow shined behind her, lighting her golden hair like it was made of fire.

"Hi" he mouthed the word, but no sound came out. His throat burst into flames at the very act of trying to speak.

"Shh," she said, and put her index finger over his lips. "Don't talk, just listen." He nodded, never taking his eyes from her perfect, beautiful face.

"I don't want to have to come down here again Jason Stevens," she said to him. He nodded again. "I want you to forgive yourself now. I've already forgiven you, but the rest is up to you." He didn't say a word, but tears streamed from his eyes as he kept them intently focused on Sarah.

"I need you to know that I'm exactly where I'm supposed to be," she explained. "I'm happy... and it's time you were too. Ok?" she smiled at him again and watched him with love as he nodded.

"Ok, good. I have to go now, but I'll be around if you need me," she leaned down and kissed him gently on his forehead. The tears flowed freely now, but not because of pain or despair. They flowed because of the freedom he was given, freedom from his prison of guilt.

Sarah stepped back from Jason and smiled one last time. A brilliant flash of light took Sarah back to her home in *Salvation City*, leaving Jason alone to reflect on the second chance at life he had been given from the woman whose life he had taken away.

Ironic...

Jason's parents came in to see him just moments after Sarah's departure. He looked at them and felt so ashamed that he had been so selfish. What would have happened to them if he had succeeded? He didn't want to know.

They both came to his side and leaned down to hold their son. This family cried together for what seemed like an eternity, but they never spoke a word to each other. They didn't need to. They were each aware of the second chance they had been given. And they fully intended to use that chance wisely.

CHAPTER 30

Now that Jason was safe, Sarah's mind was filled with dread over Vinchetto's and Calista's fate. Calista had died to save her, and Vinchetto almost met the same end. How could she ever make this right? What would she do without Calista? She loved that girl like a sister! How could this have happened?

And Vinchetto... *Vinnie the Bull...* she never thought that any of the vile spawns of Satan would be able to take him down like that. Never underestimate the power of hate... Nadira really drove that point home.

She walked into their congregation room to find Nigel and Maggie waiting for her there. She looked around, but no Vinchetto... or Calista.

"Congratulations Sarah," greeted Maggie with a smile. "I heard you saved the kid."

"Yeah, I didn't think he was going to make it at first," she confessed. "But I think he's going to be ok now."

"You did good kid... you did good," said Maggie and she nodded at Sarah in approval. Nigel hadn't said a word; he just watched her and smiled.

"Where's Vinchetto?" she asked them. Maggie and Nigel both looked at each other and smiled.

"He's on the top floor... waiting for you," answered Nigel. Sarah hurried to the main hall and levitated up to the tenth floor in search of her sparring partner. She reached the top and looked around for him. She finally spotted him in the far corner; he was sitting on the floor waiting for her. She rushed over to her friend, filled with relief that he was alright.

"Vinchetto!" she hollered at him.

"Hey there Sarah," he replied with a smile. "How's the kid?"

"He's good... he'll be fine I think... I hope. We had a nice talk before I left him." She paused and then said, "Well, I had a nice talk. He listened."

"I knew you could do it," he said.

"I wasn't so sure. For awhile I battled over whether I wanted to help him or not," she admitted reluctantly.

"Well, that's the test isn't it?" asked Vinchetto. "Not whether or not you *can* save him, but whether or not you *will* save him." He reflected for a moment and then added, "Although, saving them even when you *want* to is still pretty tough."

"I suppose," she replied.

"No *supposing* about it," he replied. "We're human Sarah; even here we'll never be perfect. We still have feelings and emotions and internal battles over what's right and what we want," he paused a moment and then continued. "Don't ever kid yourself about how hard our job here really is. For Heavenly Father's *angels* it's easier, they are born to do *His* will, we *human* redeemers are still ruled by our gift of *free will*."

"Wow," she thought this over, finally understanding the depth of their purpose. She knew what they did was important to the souls they saved, but it was equally important to their own salvation. Whether they earned their redemption or not, the tests they were given pulled them closer to Heavenly Father.

"Are we going to practice?" she asked.

"Nope."

"No? Then what are we doing up here?" she asked him.

"I just wanted to talk to you and see how you were doing after that assignment," he answered.

"That's all?" she replied in confusion.

"Well... that; and someone wanted to surprise you," he said and smiled. "Turn around." Sarah turned around to face the balcony and saw someone fly past the top floor, beautiful wings open in full, shining glory.

The angel flew all the way up to the stained glass ceiling and then around the perimeter of the top floor, but Sarah couldn't see this angel's face yet. She looked over at Vinchetto, but he just smiled as he watched this beautiful display of flight. This angel unveiling their new wings to all who would watch.

Finally the angel was heading their way. As they flew closer, Sarah could finally see who it was that was brandishing these beautiful wings.

It was Calista.

Sarah gasped and put her hand to her mouth in total awe. She was so happy that Calista wasn't gone that she was completely speechless. Calista landed softly next to them and tucked her beautiful new wings back into their typical form, a floor length, dark grey trench coat.

"Well," she said to Sarah. "Aren't you going to say something?"

"What... how? I don't know what to say," she wrapped her arms around Calista and hugged her as tight as she could.

"Well, you know that whole getting *sliced in half* thing?" Calista asked.

"Uh... yeah," replied Sarah, still in shock.

"Well, it turns out that sacrificing myself was a pretty good way to earn my redemption."

"That is so awesome! I'm so happy for you," she stopped for a moment and her tone changed a bit. "Wait a minute; aren't you going to cross over now?"

"No way!" she replied without hesitation. "My family is here. I don't have anyone in Heaven. Besides, you've inspired me to get tougher. Heck, if you can take out Nadira, just think what I could do... in a hundred years or so... and with a whole lot of practice." She laughed at herself.

"You're better than you think kiddo, I've seen you kick some serious demon butt," claimed Vinchetto.

"Yeah, I guess I have, huh?" Calista smiled at herself.

"Definitely!" added Sarah. She always knew that Calista could be one tough warrior; she just had to get over her fear. She had already faced her ultimate fear of annihilation, and she seemed to weather that just fine. The rest would be a cake walk.

"How *did* you come back?" Sarah asked, confused. "I thought Nadira killed you." Calista and Vinchetto both chuckled at the question.

"We're already dead kiddo," explained Vinchetto. "The only thing they can really do to hurt us is to persuade us to do something to cause our *fall from grace.*"

"And that doesn't happen very often," added Calista.

"Well then, where did you go? What happened to you?" Sarah questioned.

"I came back here," she replied casually. "I just couldn't go back to the assignment again. It took awhile for my energy to kinda 'recharge' again too."

"Well, that's good information to have... *can't be killed,*" Sarah noted. "That puts a whole new spin on things, doesn't it?"

"Sure does," replied Vinchetto. "It's always good to know you're invincible."

211

Nigel floated up to the tenth floor and landed right beside this inseparable trio. They stopped their conversation as they looked up at Nigel and greeted him.

"Sarah, David is here to see you," he informed her.

"Me?" she asked. "Well, it's about time he came to check on me, I thought he forgot all about me." Calista and Vinchetto glanced over at each other and smirked. The four of them levitated over the balcony and lowered themselves down to the main hall.

David was standing in the center of the main hall, waiting patiently with his hands clasped behind his back. He was smiling at Sarah.

His tie was robin's egg blue.

CHAPTER 31

The entire team was standing around David, waiting eagerly for him to state his business with Sarah. She watched him with reluctant eyes, fearing she had failed her first assignment and trying desperately to imagine what would be required of her to fix it.

He finally spoke.

"Sarah," he started. "As you know, you were brought here to earn your redemption for the horrible sin you committed against yourself... and Heavenly Father."

"Yes," she whispered, and then lowered her head in shame. He gently lifted up her chin and looked into her eyes.

"Well," he smiled at her with his perfect, game show host smile and said, "I just want to tell you that you have earned the privilege to cross over into Heaven and be with your family for all eternity... That is, if you so choose to."

"What? Really?" she was completely paralyzed, glued to the spot where she now stood. It had seemed like such an unreachable dream for so long. To be with her family again was all she wanted, and now it was real.

Very real.

The golden doors at the west end of the main hall began to open. Sarah always thought these doors led into Heaven, and now it appears that she was right.

Pure white light spilled through the opening, growing brighter as the doors opened wider. Redeeming souls from everywhere stopped what they were doing to watch. They all knew that someone would be crossing over soon.

In the distance Sarah could barely make out the faint outline of figures moving through the light toward the open door. There appeared to be two shapes... no, three shapes moving closer to the threshold. She squinted her eyes, attempting to focus on the shapes that would soon be unveiled.

She moved closer to the door.

The shapes crossed over the threshold and broke through the blinding light, revealing themselves to every watching soul in *Salvation City*. Two men and a small boy entered into *Salvation City* to claim the soul that they had left behind.

Sarah covered her mouth with her hand, completely overwhelmed with the love for the family that she so desperately needed. She walked toward them, still in disbelief.

She walked faster now... not fast enough; she broke out into a run.

When she reached her long awaiting family she dropped to her knees and threw her arms around Joey and sobbed uncontrollably. Will and Poppy knelt down and wrapped their arms around their long, lost Sarah. A broken family brought together once again.

"Hi pumpkin," said Poppy through tearful eyes. "You did it baby!" Sarah nodded, unable to speak and still holding on to her family for dear life... *her* life.

Poppy and Will let go of her and stood up. David had joined them; he had more to tell Sarah. She released the grip on her baby boy and stood up with the others. She looked at Will and he grabbed her by the hand and kissed her cheek. Tears were rolling down her face.

"Sarah," said David. "As you know, *free will* is still yours... even now." She looked at him and nodded her head in acknowledgement. "You have a choice to stay here, or cross over and be with your family."

Will, Joey, Poppy, David, Vinchetto, Nigel... the entire population of *Salvation City*, all watched her in complete silence as she looked around at all the loving faces. Her *mortal family* and her *Heavenly family*... here together as one.

Sarah knew that she would have a choice when the time came, but she was so focused on Will and Joey that she never imagined this decision would actually be this hard. She looked up at the other floors and saw a sea of faces peering over the edge, watching her and waiting anxiously for her decision.

"Will," she whispered softly.

"Yes babe?" he replied. Oh how she had longed to hear his voice again, to hear him call to her and touch her. She missed him so badly.

"I need to say goodbye to my friends... my family."

"Of course. Whatever you decide, Joey and I will be waiting here when you're ready," he said as he touched her cheek. "We have eternity you know."

She nodded and slowly walked over to her team. She was crying as she approached her beloved family of redeeming souls, her fellow warriors, her dearest friends.

"Don't even say it kid," claimed Vinchetto. He had tears in his eyes, but refused to let them fall. "Just because you're crossing over doesn't mean you're not an *angel of redemption* anymore. Don't be too proud to come back here and see us."

"What did you say?" she asked, stopping dead in her tracks.

"I said, 'don't even say it kid'," he repeated.

"Not that part, the part about coming back," her face lit up with excitement.

"What about it?" asked Vinchetto.

"Can I come back whenever I want?"

"What have I been telling you all this time? *Free will...* it's *His* gift!" claimed Vinchetto as if he was teaching a student that just wouldn't pay attention. She looked around at the group... Nigel, Maggie, Calista and David all nodded in agreement.

"Well, why didn't anyone tell me that before?" she felt just like a kid at Christmas. She couldn't believe that she would be able to stay with her family and still be an *angel of redemption.*

"Go on kid... get out of here already!" yelled out Maggie in her raspy voice.

217

"Yeah Sarah, this is what you've been waiting for," Calista added.

She looked at them one last time and turned to David, "Ok, I'm ready."

"Excellent!" he motioned to her waiting family. "All you have to do is go through the doors and you'll be home."

She took Joey and Will each by the hand and the four of them headed slowly back toward the golden doors. The bright light still hid Heaven from her view.

"Are you coming home now mommy?" asked Joey.

"Yes baby... I'm coming home."

They walked across the threshold and disappeared into the bright light of Heaven. The doors slowly closed, sealing this family within them... together for eternity.

Epilogue

Jason lay on the operating table. He was shivering, it was so cold and he was only covered by a thin hospital sheet. He couldn't see much around him, but he could hear the doctors and nurses talking. They were making casual small talk and one of them told a joke about a horse named Friday. He would have to remember that one when he woke up.

"Ok Jason, I want you to count backwards from ten," said a masked man with a blue shower cap on his head. He had the greenest eyes Jason had ever seen, and they wrinkled up at the corners when he talked.

The man with the green eyes put a breathing mask on Jason's mouth and nose. The gas that was coming from it had a funny smell.

"Ten... nine... *Sarah*," Jason said, as he faded from consciousness.

ζ

"Hi Jason," said Sarah. She was so beautiful, more beautiful than he had remembered her back in his room that awful night. The night that changed his life... again.

"Sarah," he replied. "What are you doing here? Am I dreaming?"

"Yes, you are," she answered. "Come with me, I want to show you something." She took Jason by the hand and led him into a green field of grass with blooming spring flowers. She was wearing a white summer dress that gently flowed in the soft breeze. He didn't understand what he was doing here, or why Sarah was with him.

They walked only a little bit before the grass changed into a small neighborhood street... his street. His house was just ahead on the left and they headed straight toward it. They walked through the front door as it magically opened before them. Jason could hear his parents laughing and talking in the kitchen.

As they turned the corner into the kitchen Jason could see his parents. They were they talking and laughing with him... and he *was standing. He looked around for his wheelchair, but it was nowhere to be found. He stood in silence at the sight of himself using his legs again. He hoped it would happen someday, but he kept himself prepared for the worst.*

"I've got more to show you," she took him by the hand and led him out of the house.

They were on a college campus now. There were students everywhere, scrambling to get to their classes on time. They weaved their way through the crowds as they walked toward a bench with a lone young man sitting there reading, a stack of books occupying the empty space next to him.

A pretty, young girl walked up and asked, "Is this seat taken?"

The young man looked up from his book, surprised by the interruption and replied, "No, please sit down." He quickly moved the books to the ground and started a conversation with the pretty, young girl.

The young man was Jason.

He looked again at Sarah, she didn't breathe a word to him... she only smiled. She was still holding his hand as they turned away from the blooming young couple and the daylight turned into night.

They were walking toward an outdoor garden with tiny white Christmas lights strung along a pergola and every tree surrounding the garden patio. As they drew near, Jason could see a couple dancing in the center of the patio while everyone watched with wide smiles and happy faces.

It was Jason and the pretty, young girl from the bench at the college campus. It was their wedding day... and he was dancing. Jason couldn't believe what he was seeing. He never thought that these things, this ordinary life unfolding before him would ever be within his reach.

He had spent so much time punishing himself for what he had done to the Bradley family that he didn't believe he deserved these things.

A wife... children... to walk again. All these things had been nothing more than a dream to Jason. But here they were, his future laid out before him by his guardian angel.... Sarah Bradley.

He turned to this beautiful angel of mercy and asked her, "What will you have me do Sarah?"

"Live Jason," she touched his face and kissed his cheek. "I want you to really live."

Jason closed his eyes and he could feel the warm tears streaming down his cheeks. When he opened his eyes, Sarah was gone. The wedding scene began to pull away from him, disappearing into the distance until it was nothing more than a tiny spec of light.

He was alone.

ζ

The pain was only a slight twinge at first, but it soon grew into an unbearable stabbing pain in the middle of his back. He was fading in and out of consciousness, the pain trying to wake him, but the anesthesia trying to pull him back into a deep slumber.

His stomach started to retch and he could feel himself gagging on something... it was his own vomit. Where was he? He was creeping back into consciousness now... he was in the hospital. He remembered being in the operating room, counting backwards from ten.

Sarah!

Everything came back to him now. Sarah, the field of flowers, the girl, his wedding... it was all just a dream.

"Look who's awake!" said his nurse. She pulled off his oxygen mask and wiped the vomit from his face. She had a bowl with her in case he had more stomach contents that he wanted to get rid of.

"How's your pain level?" she asked him. He held up his two hands showing all ten fingers.

"Wow! That's pretty high. Don't worry sweetheart, I'll make you feel better in no time." She pushed some fluid into his IV and the pain slowly subsided to a tolerable level, without putting him back into a coma.

He looked around the room. Standing in the corner was a beautiful woman wearing a white summer dress. She smiled at him and blew him a kiss.

He rubbed his eyes and looked again, but she was gone. It wasn't a dream, she was here... Sarah was with him again in his most desperate hour.

She was... and always will be... an angel.

His angel...

ANGELS OF REDEMPTION

ALETHEA J SALAZAR

alethea@theangelsofredemption.com

225

Made in the USA
San Bernardino, CA
04 March 2017